What was going on here?

Valerie's mouth dropped open. Stocks and bonds...six hundred shares...mineral rights leases... Edwin had been wealthy! She thought of the cheap haircuts she'd given him, of the flowers Sierra had sold him at cost, of the inflated prices Avis had paid him for his coins, and all the while the old fox had been sitting on a fortune!

"In the total amount of five million seven hundred fifty-four thousand six hundred seventy-three dollars and twenty-two cents, plus accurable interests, to named heirs...

"Valerie Blunt, Sierra Carlton and Avis Lorimer."

Valerie blinked, not understanding, not daring to understand, what she'd just heard. It finally sunk in when the attorney removed his glasses and announced gently, "Congratulations, ladies. After taxes, I'd say you've inherited just over a million dollars each."

D1414777

Dear Reader,

Well, the new year is upon us—and if you've resolved to read some wonderful books in 2004, you've come to the right place. We'll begin with *Expecting!* by Susan Mallery, the first in our five-book MERLYN COUNTY MIDWIVES miniseries, in which residents of a small Kentucky town find love—and scandal—amidst the backdrop of a midwifery clinic. In the opening book, a woman returning to her hometown, pregnant and alone, finds herself falling for her high school crush—now all grown up and married to his career! Or so he thinks....

Annette Broadrick concludes her SECRET SISTERS trilogy with *MacGowan Meets His Match.* When a woman comes to Scotland looking for a job *and* the key to unlock the mystery surrounding her family, she finds both—with the love of a lifetime thrown in!—in the Scottish lord who hires her. In *The Black Sheep Heir,* Crystal Green wraps up her KANE'S CROSSING miniseries with the story of the town outcast who finds in the big, brooding stranger hiding out in her cabin the soul mate she'd been searching for.

Karen Rose Smith offers the story of an about-to-be single mom and the handsome hometown hero who makes her wonder if she doesn't have room for just one more male in her life, in *Their Baby Bond.* THE RICHEST GALS IN TEXAS, a new miniseries by Arlene James, in which three blue-collar friends inherit a million dollars—each!—opens with *Beautician Gets Million-Dollar Tip!* A hairstylist inherits that wad just in time to bring her salon up to code, at the insistence of the infuriatingly handsome, if annoying, local fire marshal. And in Jen Safrey's *A Perfect Pair,* a woman who enlists her best (male) friend to help her find her Mr. Right suddenly realizes he's right there in front of her face—i.e., said friend! Now all she has to do is convince *him* of this....

So bundle up, and happy reading. And come back next month for six new wonderful stories, all from Silhouette Special Edition.

Sincerely,

Gail Chasan
Senior Editor

Please address questions and book requests to:
Silhouette Reader Service
U.S.: 3010 Walden Ave., P.O. Box 1325, Buffalo, NY 14269
Canadian: P.O. Box 609, Fort Erie, Ont. L2A 5X3

Beautician Gets Million-Dollar Tip!

ARLENE JAMES

SPECIAL EDITION®

Published by Silhouette Books

America's Publisher of Contemporary Romance

If you purchased this book without a cover you should be aware that this book is stolen property. It was reported as "unsold and destroyed" to the publisher, and neither the author nor the publisher has received any payment for this "stripped book."

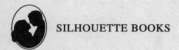

SILHOUETTE BOOKS

ISBN 0-373-24589-0

BEAUTICIAN GETS MILLION-DOLLAR TIP!

Copyright © 2004 by Deborah Rather

All rights reserved. Except for use in any review, the reproduction or utilization of this work in whole or in part in any form by any electronic, mechanical or other means, now known or hereafter invented, including xerography, photocopying and recording, or in any information storage or retrieval system, is forbidden without the written permission of the editorial office, Silhouette Books, 233 Broadway, New York, NY 10279 U.S.A.

All characters in this book have no existence outside the imagination of the author and have no relation whatsoever to anyone bearing the same name or names. They are not even distantly inspired by any individual known or unknown to the author, and all incidents are pure invention.

This edition published by arrangement with Harlequin Books S.A.

® and TM are trademarks of Harlequin Books S.A., used under license. Trademarks indicated with ® are registered in the United States Patent and Trademark Office, the Canadian Trade Marks Office and in other countries.

Visit Silhouette at www.eHarlequin.com

Printed in U.S.A.

Books by Arlene James

Silhouette Special Edition

A Rumor of Love #664
Husband in the Making #776
With Baby in Mind #869
Child of Her Heart #964
*The Knight, the Waitress
  and the Toddler* #1131
Every Cowgirl's Dream #1195
Marrying an Older Man #1235
Baby Boy Blessed #1285
Her Secret Affair #1421
His Private Nurse #1482
**Beautician Gets Million-Dollar Tip!* #1589

Silhouette Romance

City Girl #141
No Easy Conquest #235
Two of a Kind #253
A Meeting of Hearts #327
An Obvious Virtue #384
Now or Never #404
Reason Enough #421
The Right Moves #446
Strange Bedfellows #471
The Private Garden #495
The Boy Next Door #518
Under a Desert Sky #559
A Delicate Balance #578
The Discerning Heart #614
Dream of a Lifetime #661
Rumor of Love #664
Finally Home #687
A Perfect Gentleman #705
Family Man #728
A Man of His Word #770
Tough Guy #806

Silhouette Books

Fortune's Children
Single with Children

The Fortunes of Texas
Corporate Daddy

Gold Digger #830
Palace City Prince #866
**The Perfect Wedding* #962
**An Old-Fashioned Love* #968
**A Wife Worth Waiting For* #974
Mail-Order Brood #1024
**The Rogue Who Came To Stay* #1061
**Most Wanted Dad* #1144
Desperately Seeking Daddy #1186
**Falling for a Father of Four* #1295
A Bride To Honor #1330
Mr. Right Next Door #1352
Glass Slipper Bride #1379
A Royal Masquerade #1432
In Want of a Wife #1466
The Mesmerizing Mr. Carlyle #1493
So Dear To My Heart #1535
The Man with the Money #1592

*This Side of Heaven
**The Richest Gals in Texas

ARLENE JAMES

grew up in Oklahoma and has lived all over the South.
In 1976 she married "the most romantic man in the world."
The author enjoys traveling with her husband, but writing
has always been her chief pastime. Arlene is also the author
of the inspirational titles *Proud Spirit, A Wish for Always,
Partners for Life* and *No Stranger to Love.*

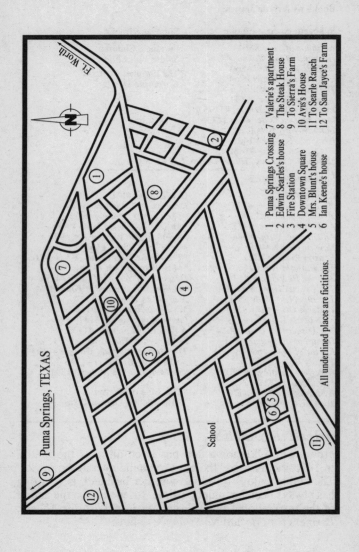

Puma Springs, TEXAS

Fl. Worth

N

1 Puma Springs Crossing
2 Edwin Searles's house
3 Fire Station
4 Downtown Square
5 Mrs. Blunt's house
6 Ian Keene's house
7 Valerie's apartment
8 The Steak House
9 To Sierra's Farm
10 Avis's House
11 To Searle Ranch
12 To Sam Jayce's Farm

School

All underlined places are fictitious.

Chapter One

"No, no, no!" Edwin Searle scowled at his reflection in the mirror and plucked at the side of his head with blunt, gnarled fingers. "You still don't got it."

"And you," Valerie said patiently as she combed up the already short, silver hair in the area indicated, "have the eyes of an eagle since you had those cataracts removed." She applied the humming razor so judiciously that it would have taken a microscope to measure what she'd cut away, but the grizzled old cowboy actually smiled—before he poked at another spot.

"Right there."

Ducking her head, Valerie dutifully combed up another section and deftly wielded her electric razor. Edwin was her most irascible customer. He visited her shop every other Thursday and always grumbled about the five-dollar haircut. They went through it hair-by-hair every time, but Val had long ago deduced that Edwin was not picky so much as he was simply interested in prolonging his time in her chair. For all his scowls and grumbles, Edwin Searle was a lonely old man reaching out the best way he knew how. She could take a little extra time with him.

Besides, the customers weren't exactly lining up around the block today, not that they ever did. Operating her own beauty and barber shop had not turned out quite as Valerie had expected. Oh, she had a loyal following, enough to keep the regular bills paid, but with a population of 8,000, Puma Springs was too small and too close to Fort Worth to reward its small businesses with more than subsistence income. She held her breath every month, praying nothing unusual would crop up, but as often as not, it did.

Just this week she'd received notice that her irresponsible younger brother had again failed a university class, wasting the tuition she'd paid out. Without that class, Dillon could not graduate, and if Valerie didn't come up with the extra tuition for him to repeat it, her widowed mother would have to. That Val couldn't bear.

With an inward sigh, Valerie combed down this last section of hair and stood back, razor running, while Edwin made a study of his head in the mirror. Before he could pick a hair to complain about, the shop door opened, capturing Valerie's attention for an instant. Her smile of greeting faltered as her erstwhile boyfriend, Buddy Wilcox, slimed into the room.

"Hey."

Without returning the greeting, Valerie turned back to Edwin. Buddy was a bad habit that Valerie was determined to break. Vain to the point of arrogance, he often dropped by unannounced for a dust-up or styling of his thick, sandy-brown hair, for which he rarely paid. She'd let him get away with it in the past, but no more. She had finally become immune to those pale blue eyes.

Valerie and Buddy had dated intermittently since high school, when she'd been homecoming queen and he had stood as captain of the football team, the Puma Springs Panthers. This was not what had repeatedly revived the relationship, however. That could be chalked up to the lack of other options around town. Soon after graduation, nearly all of their contemporaries had either married quickly, headed off to college or migrated elsewhere. Permanently.

Valerie herself had temporarily relocated to Fort Worth to train as a hairstylist and cosmetologist, but she'd always planned on returning to Puma Springs to be near her widowed mother and younger brother. Buddy had never left and never intended to. He was quite content to drift from low-wage job to low-wage job, dining out on his reputation as the town's most successful high school football quarterback. At twenty-four, Val felt that she had finally grown up. Buddy never would.

''What do you want, Bud? I don't have time to do your hair.''

''Take another look, sugar,'' Buddy retorted, strolling toward the mirror to check himself out. ''My hair looks great.''

Edwin humphed and shifted in his chair. Knowing that Buddy would get around to the purpose of his visit eventually, Valerie began combing up possible targets for her razor. Sure enough, Buddy turned abruptly and blurted it out.

"I need your car."

Valerie automatically glanced over her shoulder through the plate glass window at the four-year-old, black, domestic coupe parked in front of the strip mall where she rented shop space. She still owed two years on the note and had just repaired the dent that her reckless brother had put in the passenger door. Compared to Buddy, Dillon was as careful as the examiner down at the Department of Public Safety. Shutting off the razor, she laid it aside and folded her arms.

"In your dreams."

"Come on, Val," Buddy whined.

"No way. You drive like you're on a NASCAR track."

He grinned cheekily. "Thanks."

"It wasn't a compliment."

"Look, this is important, Val. I don't have time to argue with you. Keys on the hook?" Ignoring her glower, he strode for the back of the shop.

"Get back here!" she yelled, starting after him. "I didn't say you could—"

The door opened again, and Valerie momentarily forgot about Buddy Wilcox and the potential threat to her car as a tall, good-looking man and his big, black dog strolled in. The man was broad-shouldered with thick, pitch-black hair, strong jaw and straight white teeth. The dog, too, was larger than normal, a model of his breed, but while the dog obediently sat on command and stared up at her with a gaze as black as its coat, the man smiled down, his vivid, electric blue eyes inquisitive—and just a shade appreciative.

"Are you…" He consulted the clipboard in his hand. "Valerie Blunt?"

"Ah. Yes, actually, I am."

He shifted the clipboard and stuck out a hand the size of a shoe box. "I'm Ian Keene, the new fire marshal."

Fire marshal. She'd read about him in the local weekly. Word was that he came highly decorated and qualified, but the editorial page argued that he was too expensive, especially since he'd brought an assistant chief with him. Nevertheless, the town council had unanimously voted to hire the Fort Worth native, citing a state study that had placed the small community in the center of an area prone to wildfire danger. Two years of drought, followed by an unusually dry winter, had robbed the early spring of much of its green, leaving the thick grass brittle and prickly and driving the local ranchers to truck in mountains of hay to feed their herds.

While the paper had trumpeted the new marshal's heroism and qualifications, it had said nothing about the way he filled out that red flannel shirt and those snug new jeans. Paul Bunyan couldn't have done better. His firm, warm, long-fingered hand literally swallowed hers. He didn't look as if he needed a haircut, but she couldn't think of another reason why he'd be there.

"What can I do for you, Marshal Keene?"

He tilted his head and took his hand back. "I'm here to inspect the place."

"Inspect," she echoed stupidly. At that moment, Buddy strode out of the shop, her keys in his hand.

"Found them," he announced, which meant he'd rifled through her purse because she hadn't hung them on the hook. His reason for "dropping by" resurfaced in her now-spinning head.

"Buddy, don't you dare—"

"Inspect!" Edwin suddenly erupted. Valerie swung a distracted glance in his direction. "I knew no good would come of this fire marshal business."

Puzzled, she looked to the newcomer for clarification and spotted Buddy sliding behind the new fire marshal to open the door.

"See ya!" he sang out.

The fire marshal glanced over his shoulder and actually stepped forward out of Buddy's way.

"Don't!" Valerie cried, but the door was already closing behind Buddy—and her car keys. She tossed a glare at Ian Keene and rushed to the window, yelling, "Buddy!" He flipped her a wave as he dropped down behind the wheel of her car. "You'd better be back here...by closing," she finished impotently, watching her car drive away. Briefly, she closed her eyes, but her irritation could not be contained, and she whirled around in search of a target. She found a big one standing right in front of her. "Now look what you've done!"

"Me?" Ian Keene said. "I just came to inspect your shop for compliance."

"With *what?*"

''Fire code.''

''No one told me anything about a new fire code.''

''Not new,'' he corrected succinctly. ''It just hasn't been enforced until now.''

''It's Heston,'' Edwin declared, twisting around in his chair to wag a finger at the fire marshal. ''That boy don't care a fig about another human being, never has, never will, and I don't mind saying so, even if his mama is my own sister.'' He got up and fished his wallet from the back pocket of his baggy jeans.

''So you're the mayor's uncle, are you?'' Keene asked with obvious interest.

Edwin threw a five-dollar bill onto the top of the narrow cabinet below the mirror, saying, ''I'm Edwin Searle, and Callie Searle Witt's my sister, but I don't claim Heston Witt as family.'' He stomped jerkily toward the hat rack beside the door, muttering, ''Grasping, greedy, full of hisself.'' He paused to scratch the head of the dog still sitting obediently before its master, then clumped over to the brass hat tree in his scuffed boots to retrieve his battered, sweat-stained cowboy hat. ''This here inspection nonsense is just Heston throwing his weight around.''

''Actually,'' the fire marshal said, ''the city council made these inspections mandatory. The mayor was the only one against it.''

''You mean he ain't set you up for inspecting my place?'' Edwin demanded.

''Well, he did mention that there might be some problems out your way,'' Keene admitted mildly.

Edwin straightened his stooped shoulders and

shook a blunt, crooked finger in the fire marshal's face. "You ain't setting foot on my property."

"Oh, but I am," Keene replied with easy authority, "and if changes need to be made, they will be."

"Over my dead body!" Edwin growled, yanking open the door.

"That's just what we're trying to avoid with these inspections," Keene told him calmly. Edwin made his opinion of that sentiment plain by stepping through the door and snapping it closed with a rude snort.

Ian Keene shook his head before turning his neon blue gaze on Valerie again. "He always that pleasant?"

She quickly assessed the big man and came to several conclusions. Ian Keene was confident to the point of arrogance and too good-looking by half. And, she thought mulishly, he'd let Buddy get away with her car.

"Edwin can be difficult," she admitted, "especially if you harangue him."

"Seemed to me he was the one doing the haranguing," Keene said. He snapped his fingers then, and the dog got up and began ambling around the shop, nosing everything. Valerie frowned.

"Well, I don't think I like this inspection thing any more than Edwin does," she grumbled, her worried gaze following the sniffing dog.

Keene looked around him and made some notes on his clipboard, saying, "Got to be done. Only way to bring this town up to code and minimize the fire hazard. I'll make it quick. I have lots of work waiting."

"A really long list of people to hassle today?" she asked sweetly.

"I don't think trying to keep people safe qualifies as hassling. Now then, how many rooms do you have here?"

Valerie swallowed an acidic reply and said reluctantly, "Three, counting the storage room and the rest room."

He nodded, made a note and began wandering around. "You just go about your business. I'll be out of your hair in a few minutes. No pun intended."

She folded her arms to let him know that she wasn't amused and impatiently tapped her toe as he moved from cabinet to cabinet and corner to corner.

He inspected the chair, as if that might burst into flame at any moment, then moved on to the washing station. The electric wall heater got such a thorough going over that she rolled her eyes—and as she did, she caught sight of his dog slinking around the corner into the back room.

"Would you get your dog in hand? What do you mean bringing a dog into a place of business anyway?"

"Cato's a vital part of the process," the fire marshal said, following her line of sight before informing her smartly, "I'll need to see where you store your bulk supplies. Beauty products contain a fair amount of alcohol and other combustibles."

As if she didn't know that.

The dog *whuffed* then, and Keene suddenly turned away, heading toward the back of the shop. Valerie followed right on his heels.

"Ah," he said, rounding the corner.

"What does that mean? Ah? It's a storage room." She tried to look past his shoulder at whatever it was that had claimed his attention, but a cold nose in her palm and a pathetic whine had her looking down at the dog instead. It promptly sat on her foot and lolled its red tongue out the side of its mouth, panting for attention. "You better not have done what I think you did," she muttered, looking for a telltale puddle. Seeing none, she gave in and patted the critter between its spiked ears. It closed its eyes in appreciation.

"Cato, strike," Ian Keene ordered. The dog picked up its warm behind and trotted over to the fire marshal, who kneeled before her new hot water tank.

Valerie folded her arms and leaned a shoulder against the door casing, flipping a hand toward the cabinet jammed into one corner. "You'll notice that the supplies are in this metal storage locker at the opposite end of the room."

He seemed to ignore her, then the dog stuck its nose behind the heater and whined. "Good boy," Ian said, patting the dog's sturdy flanks. He began twisting valves.

Valerie straightened. "What are you doing?"

"I'm shutting it off," he informed her. "You've got a gas leak."

"That's impossible! I just had this thing put in."

He shrugged and made a notation on the clipboard. "You've still got a gas leak."

She sniffed suspiciously. "I don't smell anything."

"Neither do I, but Cato does."

"You're going to let your dog shut off my hot water? I can't work without hot water!"

"I'll fix the connection before I leave," he said offhandedly, pulling out a carpenter's measuring tape. "You can work at least temporarily, but this heater's going to have to be moved." He pocketed the tape and stood.

"What?" She straightened and started forward.

"I said, you have to move your hot water heater." He walked toward the door while making a final note on his clipboard and nearly bowled her over.

She bounced off his chest, then found two strong arms steadying her. Their feet tangled, bodies met, and suddenly both froze. Heat flashed from every point where they touched, little bolts of lightning that crackled unseen in the air. For a long moment, they stood transfixed, then the clipboard slipped from his stiff fingers and clattered to the floor, breaking the spell, and they jumped apart. Valerie's hand went to her chest in an attempt to calm her racing heart, while Ian stooped, swept up the clipboard and rose again, clearing his throat.

"About four inches should do it," he muttered.

Four inches? Four inches! He was telling her, *ordering* her, to move her hot water heater four lousy inches? And at what cost? She'd already spent over a thousand bucks getting adequate hot water in here. "I can't do that!"

"I'm afraid you don't have any choice," he said, stepping around her.

"Where are you going?" she demanded, whirling

to follow him. She caught up with him just as he reached the outside door.

"I'll be right back," he assured her, heading out to the parking lot.

She threw up her hands and said a word better left unheard. A soulful whine reminded her that she was not alone. The dog stood at her side again, black eyes beguiling her. "This is all your fault," she complained. "Sniffing around people's hot water heaters. Shame on you."

He *whuffed* and reared up on his hind legs, nearly knocking her off her feet and swiping at her face with his red, doggy tongue. She smiled in spite of herself.

"Down, Cato," Keene ordered, returning at that moment with a small toolbox. The dog immediately dropped down onto all fours again, whining a protest. "He likes you," Keene commented idly, walking straight past her.

"Lucky me," she grumbled, but she gave the dog a surreptitious pat as she followed his master into the back room again. "You don't really mean that I have to move the hot water heater, do you?" she wheedled. "I just had it installed."

"Doesn't matter," he said, going down on one knee beside the offending appliance. "It wasn't installed to code." He opened his toolbox and went to work.

"That's not my fault," she argued. "I don't know anything about codes."

"Doesn't matter. I can't let it pass."

"You're really going to make me have the thing moved? For *four inches?*"

"It's either that or replace it with an electric model."

"The commercial electric rates around here are too high."

"Then bring it into code by moving it out from the wall four more inches."

"But I just had that put in!" she bawled at him, in case he hadn't gotten the message. "It's already cost me a fortune!"

"Not my problem," he said, working steadily. "Talk to your plumber. He should have done it correctly."

Valerie gaped at him. Despair mingled with a rising anger. "This isn't fair."

"What's not fair about it? Everybody's held to the same standard. Bring it into code, or I'll shut you down." He sat back on his heel and withdrew some type of meter, seemingly unaware that he had just dealt her a devastating blow.

"How can you do that?"

He looked at her. "It's my job." He placed the tools in the box, closed it, and rose. "You have ten days," he said, sliding past her once more. "I'll send around an official notice. Have a good one."

As if! Ten days. He'd given her all of ten days. She didn't know whether to laugh or cry. Closing her eyes, she tried to take in the enormity of this catastrophe. Was it possible her plumber might take a credit card? Then again, judging by what the initial installation had cost, she didn't have a large enough credit line left to cover it. She heard Ian Keene snapping his dog to heel, and then he was going out the door.

There was no way she could let him go without making her feelings fully known. Whirling around, she hurried back to the styling room, only to watch the door close on his back. Unthinkingly, she grabbed up the heaviest brush in her arsenal and flung it with all her might. The blasted thing hit the narrow metal door frame and ricocheted right back in her direction. She dodged it and watched in horror as the brush flew toward the large mirror on the wall. She winced at the inevitable clatter and tinkle of brush and glass as it hit the floor.

What was wrong with her? This wasn't how she usually dealt with her frustration, and God knew life had thrown her plenty of curves, starting when her father had died in an auto accident in the middle of her junior year in high school. Nothing really seemed to have gone right since. She might as well start looking for a chair in another shop.

Fortunately for now, anyway, she'd only broken off about a three-inch triangular section of the corner of the mirror. It wasn't pretty, but at least the whole thing hadn't shattered. No doubt it was still enough to bring down seven years of bad luck on her head. Then again, the last seven hadn't exactly been a picnic. Heavens, but she was tired of bouncing from one crisis to another. It was always about money.

Resentfully she plopped down into the styling chair and dropped her forehead onto her palm. She'd had that hot water heater installed in good faith. It wasn't her fault some petty, hard-nosed bureaucrat belatedly decided to enforce an obscure building code. How was she supposed to know how far out from the wall to set a gas hot water heater? It just wasn't fair.

It just wasn't fair.

No matter how handsome he was.

Chapter Two

"I'll just have to unplug everything," the attractive brunette said, shaking her head so that her soft, milk-chocolate hair undulated in rich waves.

At thirty-two, Avis Lorimer had been widowed almost three years. Upon the death of her husband, a retired college professor who had been more than two decades her senior, she'd taken over his small hobby shop and somehow managed to turn what had been little more than a pastime for him into a living of sorts for herself. Now Ian Keene had decreed that she either had to unplug most of her miniature trains, lighted dollhouses, knitting machines and so forth or install several more electrical circuits and outlets in her store. It didn't seem to matter to the dogged fire marshal, Valerie mused, that Avis couldn't afford new circuits or that those very products drew people into the shop.

"It's not fair," Valerie muttered. She'd been doing a slow burn ever since she'd learned of the problems the fire marshal had created for her friends.

"May not be fair," Gwyn said, refilling Val's coffee cup, "but he sure does get around. That's one serious fire marshal. Not to mention good-looking."

Gwyn Dunstan put in long days at her coffee shop, rising in the dead of night to begin making doughnuts and fancy baked goods and closing up in midafternoon. The grueling pace had rendered the thirty-six-year-old divorced mother of two "lean and mean," as her son put it, but Gwyn was not unkind so much as beaten down. Fortunately, she hadn't fared too badly with the new fire marshal, who had decreed merely that she move some shelving and rearrange her stock of combustibles.

"He may be handsome," Sierra Carlton said, "but he sure is all-business, and believe me, I did my best to distract him."

She fluttered her gold-tipped lashes and stroked the end of her long, thick braid. Gwyn and Avis laughed, but Valerie felt an unsettling spurt of...well, it had to be concern. After all, the tall, willowy redhead had fared the worst among the "gals" at the strip mall. Keene had found numerous violations in her florist's shop, and despite a personality as bright as her hair, Sierra had been subdued ever since.

The four women shared the strip mall known as the Puma Springs Crossing with an insurance agent and a chiropractor, but as married men, those two kept to themselves. The "gals," on the other hand, habitually took a break together just after Gwyn closed up the coffee shop. That way they could visit uninterrupted while keeping watchful eyes on their own businesses.

"This is going to cost real money," Valerie pointed out, just in case anyone had failed to understand the seriousness of their individual positions.

Sierra nodded. "And the only customer I had all morning was Edwin."

"Stopped in for his usual dozen carnations, did he?" Gwyn asked, lifting one hand to slide it beneath her biscuit-brown ponytail to massage her neck.

"Half for his sister," Sierra confirmed, "half for his wife's grave, as usual."

"You shouldn't sell to him at your cost," Gwyn said disapprovingly.

Sierra merely shrugged. "I can't help it. The poor old thing obviously doesn't have two nickels to rub together."

Gwyn snorted at that. "He's probably got the first nickel he ever earned."

"Well, if he does, it's probably worth a pretty penny," Avis put in. "I've bought more old coins from him than everyone else in town."

"And overpaid for them all, no doubt," Gwyn said, shaking her head. "I don't understand y'all. Val practically cuts his hair for free, and you two probably lose money in every transaction with him, but what's he ever done for any of you?"

"It's not about that," Valerie said. "I think it's sweet that he's so devoted to visiting his sister in the nursing home and tending his late wife's grave."

"Sweet is the last word I'd use in connection with that ornery old goat," Gwyn muttered. "He probably treated them both like dirt before and just buys them flowers because he's got a guilty conscience now."

"You don't know that," Avis pointed out gently.

"Stands to reason," Gwyn argued. "He's a man, isn't he?"

"Oh, come on, Gwyn," Avis said softly. "We all know you occasionally give him an extra bun or cup of coffee."

Gwyn bristled at the mere suggestion. "Only if it'd be thrown out otherwise."

The three women sitting around the small rectangular table traded knowing looks and sipped their beverages, none of which they'd paid for.

"Well, anyway," Val said, "Edwin Searle is not the problem here. The problem is Ian Keene."

Avis folded her arms. "The way I see it, the city council is at fault. They should have grandfathered in those of us who opened before the new building codes went into effect."

"That's the problem," Gwyn said. "These aren't *new* building codes. It's just that nobody ever bothered to enforce them before."

"So, like I said," Valerie persisted, "this is all Ian Keene's fault."

"He certainly has put me in a pickle," Sierra said. "I just don't know what I'm going to do."

"Well, you can't blame the man for doing his job," Gwyn said.

"I can," Val admitted bluntly. No matter how handsome the man might be, he had to understand that he was mucking around with people's livelihoods, and she was just the gal to deliver the message. Move this. Replace that. More of something, less of another. Who did he think he was anyway? Narrowing her eyes, she decided aloud, "Maybe it's time someone put a bug in our mayor's ear, let him know the voting citizens of Puma Springs are not best pleased."

"Can't hurt," Sierra said, looking up. Valerie looked at Avis for agreement, and after a split-second hesitation, that dark head nodded solemnly. Val's frosty smile denoted her pleasure.

"I'll see him this afternoon, then."

"Go on," Gwyn said skeptically, "for all the good it'll do you. Waste of breath if you ask me, but then, that's about all any of us have to spare."

And that, Valerie decided, was just the point.

"Are you sure they're planning legal action?" Avis asked.

Valerie glanced at each of the three women clustered about the coffee shop table and shrugged. Her visit with the mayor had not gone well. Heston Witt was a soft, oily, self-important little man who didn't have the sense to realize that he'd maintained his seat in office because the citizenry considered him harmless. The city council repeatedly endorsed him because he was too lazy and inept to get in their way. Still, on occasion he could be stirred to take a stand. Not, however, when it came to Ian Keene.

"All I know is that the fire marshal has the unqualified support of the mayor and has been empowered by the city council to instigate legal action for noncompliance of code. Heston cited Edwin as an example of someone who might be a problem, and he described Edwin's place as an eyesore and a hazard.''

Avis slid a worried look around the table and asked, ''What can we do?''

''I guess we could help Edwin clean up his place,'' Valerie suggested.

Sierra took a deep breath and nodded. ''Might as well. Helping someone else might get our minds off our own troubles. It'd certainly give old Heston a nasty shock.''

''Will Edwin let us help him, though?'' Avis asked.

''We just won't give him any option,'' Val said firmly.

''I bet he'll be grateful for the help,'' Sierra said.

Gwyn just shook her head. ''Edwin Searle grateful? That'll be the day. You do understand that this isn't a feather-dusters-and-rubber-gloves kind of job? There's enough junk piled up around his place to fill a train car.''

''Does that mean you won't be helping us?'' Val asked flatly.

''It does,'' Gwyn answered in the same tone.

''It wouldn't be fair to expect her to,'' Avis pointed out. ''She's up at three every morning and has two teenagers to worry about.''

''Could you watch Tyree for me, then?'' Sierra pleaded of Gwyn. ''It'll have to be Sunday since that's our only day off. Surely we won't be at Edwin's past dark.''

''You won't be at Edwin's for ten minutes,'' Gwyn

predicted dryly, ''but I'll watch the girl for you long as you need. And since you're dead set on sticking your noses into old man Searle's business, let me tell you what I heard this morning.''

She went on to describe how the new fire marshal had been seen accompanying Edwin into a local attorney's office and then to the bank.

''We may be too late,'' Avis said, looking from Val to Sierra and back again. ''Sounds like Edwin might have already paid a fine or something.''

''Don't those types of fines usually work on a daily basis?'' Val asked. ''Every day that you don't comply it's another fine?''

''There's more,'' Gwyn went on. ''Doesn't make a lot of sense to me, but I have it on good authority that Keene was seen later taking things from the Searle place, boxes and suitcases, they said.''

Valerie looked at her friends in alarm. ''You don't suppose that they're trying to put poor Edwin away?''

''It's not that,'' Gwyn stated.

Val drew her brows together. ''How do you know?''

Gwyn shrugged one shoulder negligently. ''I asked.''

''You asked the fire marshal about it?'' Sierra demanded.

''I was polite,'' Gwyn said defensively, ''and he politely refused to answer, except to say that Edwin wasn't being forced out of his home.''

Valerie frowned. ''Edwin still needs help, and I'm willing to give it a shot.''

The other two volunteers nodded, and it was settled. Val smiled grimly. It would do nothing about their own situations, but at least Ian Keene wouldn't have Edwin Searle to push around anymore.

Valerie tugged the brim of her battered felt hat lower over her eyebrows. A relic from her high school drill team days, the poor old thing was woefully out of style and more gray than white now, but it still got the job done. One of these days she was going to buy a new hat. Maybe she'd buy a new pair of boots, too. She scoffed inwardly. Fat chance. Not only did she have tuition to pay and a hot water heater to move, Buddy had returned her car with the rear side panel caved in. She was about as likely to get new boots and a hat as she was to hit the lottery without buying a ticket.

Sierra reached out and again clanged the cow bell fixed to the fence post beside the gate, giving it a good, long shake this time.

"Hold your horses!" Edwin rasped from beyond the tall wood fence.

Valerie traded nervous glances with Sierra and Avis. Sierra turned her ball cap around backward, while Avis patted the simple scarf tied over her dark, lustrous hair. The gate creaked open a moment later, and Edwin stuck his gray head out. Surprise registered on his seamed face, and the gate abruptly swung wider.

"What in tarnation are you three doing here?"

As the instigator of this scene, Val felt she ought to take the lead. Smiling brightly, she chirruped, "We heard you needed some help cleaning up the place."

Edwin frowned. "What? Was it broadcast over the radio? I swear, a man's got no privacy around this here town." He stepped back and roughly motioned for them to follow him. "Come on then. Day's half gone already."

The women traded bemused looks and one by one stepped through the gate onto an overgrown path. Valerie felt movement at her side and glanced down to find a dog at her side, a big dog. A big, vaguely familiar, black dog. She didn't know Edwin owned a pet. She patted the broad head absently as it rubbed against her knee and followed Edwin along the path. He stepped around the thick trunk of a mature native pecan tree and addressed someone hidden by it.

"Got you some help, I reckon." He jerked a thumb over one shoulder. "I'm a popular feller these days." He shook his head before turning to beckon them closer. "He'll tell you what to do." With that, Edwin turned toward the house, the dog falling in at his side. Valerie closed her eyes, knowing intuitively who was moving around that big old tree.

"Well," Ian said. "Thanks for showing up. I wasn't expecting help."

A moment of awkward silence followed, then Sierra cleared her throat and said, "Edwin is…a good customer."

"We, uh, we've been worried about him," Avis added softly.

Valerie forced her eyes open to find Ian Keene nodding, his gaze drilling straight into hers. "Okay," he said. "That's good to hear."

While he lifted a heavily gloved hand to the back

of his neck and glanced around as if assessing the situation, Valerie quickly assessed him. The cowboy hat suited him. A natural straw, it called attention to his ink-black hair and height. The thin, simple white T-shirt and rumpled, low-slung jeans he wore as easily as he wore his skin. He seemed as at home as if he were standing in his own yard. For some reason, that rankled her. Then again, everything about the man rankled her.

He pointed in the direction from which he'd come, saying, ''Basically I'm just tossing everything into this trailer, which I'll dump down at the landfill later.''

He walked away, and the other women followed without hesitation, but a moment passed before Val could force her own feet to move. All right, she told herself, so he was helping Edwin clean up, but Ian Keene had caused the problem to begin with. Helping out was the least he could do. It didn't make him a hero—just a more decent human being than she'd thought.

She came around the tree and caught sight of a blue metal trailer hitched to a late model, dark green pickup truck. He'd cleared a path from the wide back gate in order to get the rig into the yard. Scraps of weathered lumber, broken-down furniture, downed tree limbs and barrels of half-burnt trash were scattered around a leaning garage that would probably collapse when all the debris was gone. Empty crates and sagging cardboard boxes were stacked against a rusty metal shed overflowing with cans and kegs and sacks.

"What's Edwin doing with all this junk?" Sierra wanted to know.

Ian shrugged. "I think he had some notion of re-cycling it all. He said Marge, his wife, couldn't abide waste and thought they ought to do something about all the reusable stuff folks were throwing away. My feeling is that he was more or less indulging her with plans to open a recycling center here in Puma Springs, and then when she died, his will to follow through with their plans sort of died, too."

"Poor old guy," Avis said, pulling on a pair of sturdy gardening gloves that she'd tucked into her waistband before getting out of Valerie's car.

Ian smiled. "I think he might take issue with that label, frankly. Way he tells it, he's had it all in his time."

"Looks like it's all still here, too," Sierra muttered, and Ian Keene chuckled. Intriguing little laugh lines appeared at the outside corners of his eyes and carved deep grooves in his cheeks. Valerie felt the bottom of her stomach open up.

He looked down at Sierra's bare hands then and said, "If you don't have gloves, there's an extra pair in the truck."

"Thanks," she said brightly. "I didn't think to bring any."

For the first time, Ian Keene turned to Valerie. "How about you?"

She reached behind her and tugged a brand spanking new pair of leathers from her hip pocket. "Brought my own." The words sounded clipped and icy.

Keene grinned, as if he found her animosity highly amusing. "Well, I guess you can get right to work then," he said, sweeping his gaze from the crown of her hat down to the toes of her torn boots. That grin seemed edged with derision to Valerie. He escorted the pretty redhead to the truck and opened the front door to lean inside, speaking. Sierra laughed and glanced in Val's direction with a waggle of her eyebrows before turning back to receive the gloves.

"Looks like we guessed wrong so far as Ian Keene's concerned," Avis murmured, bending to pick up a tattered wood shingle.

"Why? What is he? God's gift to grumpy old men?" Val scoffed.

Avis straightened, a look of surprise on her face. "The marshal is obviously trying to help Edwin just like we are."

"The marshal caused this whole thing," Val pointed out.

"What else could he do?" Avis asked. "Look around. One errant spark in the dry summertime and this place is an instant bonfire."

"Maybe so," Valerie muttered irritably, "but I still don't like him."

Avis slid a look over one shoulder, and Valerie followed suit. Ian Keene was leaning against the side of his truck, his hat pushed back on his head, chatting amiably with Sierra. Val's temperature shot straight through the top of her head. Suddenly Avis cut that look at Valerie.

"What's not to like, Val? The man can't be all bad

if he's here helping out. Besides, he's a genuine hunk. Genuinely single, too.''

Valerie's heart thumped so hard that she could practically see her chest move. ''So? What do I care? He's still costing me, us, a lot of money we don't have.''

Avis wilted somewhat. ''Well, it's not as if he isn't right, you know.''

Val gaped at her friend. ''Right? He's not right! He…he's a bully!''

Sierra put her head back and laughed long and loud then. Avis glanced Ian Keene's way again. ''She doesn't seem to think so.''

Suddenly Ian pushed away from the truck and began striding toward them, Sierra falling in at his side. Valerie gulped. She hadn't really looked at Sierra before. The woman's jeans were skintight, and the little top she wore hugged her lithe but generous curves with loving detail. Not liking the feeling of envy that suddenly assailed her, Val quickly turned away.

''If y'all can manage the small stuff,'' Ian called, ''Sierra and I are going to try our hands at hoisting some of this furniture.''

Sierra, Val thought bitterly. So they were on a first-name basis, were they? She began picking up trash, snatching up one piece after another, and silently cursing the day Ian Keene had ventured into Puma Springs.

Chapter Three

"Over here," Ian called. "We need some help with this."

Valerie glared venom in his direction. He felt as though he was struck every time he looked at her, like a hammer smacked an anvil and sent off sparks.

It didn't make a lot of sense. She wasn't his type, with that jagged, stripy, beauty-shop-chic haircut. He liked natural blondes with long hair and a penchant for jeans and sneakers. Valerie wore trendy, fashionable stuff, including that pale, pale lipstick that he hated. Heck, she wasn't even the best-looking woman here, though she was trying to be the most unpleasant. So what was it that continually drew his eye and kept his senses radiating?

Perhaps it was the shirt—tailored to the millimeter and outlining the fullness of her small, high breasts.

However, the pouty frown put him in mind of a spoiled child. Daddy's little princess. Somebody should have spanked that pert little bottom until she figured out that the real world wasn't about *her*.

He turned away and bent over the rusty box springs at his feet, trying to get such a grip on the thing that it wouldn't come apart the instant it was lifted. Sierra moved to his side, taking up the position she's staked out for herself, and as the other two women drew near, he directed them each to a corner.

"You can't lift by the frame. You have to find a spring with a solid link to the others and pick it up by that. Okay?" He waited until they each chose a rusty coil, then flexed his knees. "Ready? All together now. One, two, three."

The thing was heavier than it looked and remarkably unwieldy, but they seemed to have it in hand until Sierra stumbled on the way back to the trailer. Once the light steel boxframe twisted, springs started popping like firecrackers on the Fourth of July. One hit Ian under the chin, clacking his teeth together and snapping his head back. The women all dropped their grips and ran, except Sierra who went down on her knees and covered her head with her hands as metal shot through the air like ricocheting bullets. Then, as suddenly as it had begun, it was over.

Hunched and poised to dodge, they looked at one another. Everyone seemed whole, just a little stunned. About half the bed springs remained intact.

The door to the house opened, and Edwin shook his grizzled head. "Never should've tried to tighten down them springs, I reckon."

Ian blinked at him, and then instinctively he looked to Valerie. It was there, exactly what he expected, glowing in those golden-brown eyes, the perfect twin to the thought that had sprung fully formed into his own mind: only Edwin could have turned a set of bed springs at least three decades past use into a lethal weapon. Ian's mouth quirked at one corner, and so did Valerie's. Then suddenly they were both laughing.

It escalated instantly into uncontrollable guffaws and shrieks. He slapped his thigh, one foot coming up off the ground. She bent double, a fist knotted against her flat middle. They were laughing so hard, so immersed in this shared stream of ironic understanding, that he didn't realize for some time that they were the only two caught by it. He finally got a rein on it, clearing his throat, gulping in air.

Edwin was looking at him as if he'd lost his mind, and perhaps he had. "Everyone okay?" he asked.

Ian coughed. "F-fine. I think we're all…fine?"

Valerie put a hand over her mouth and literally swallowed her waning laughter. Avis and Sierra nodded, eyes tracking from Valerie to Ian to Edwin.

"One of those things shot right by my head," Avis said softly.

Sierra picked herself up and dusted herself off, taking full stock. "Just a little ping on the arm," she said in a voice taut enough to let Ian know that it had hurt.

"Better take a look," Edwin said, hitching forward. "Come on into the house and get a cool drink.

Got a pitcher of iced tea sweating all over my kitchen table.''

"Better do as he says," Ian said after clearing his throat again. "We could all use a little break, anyway." He glanced at Valerie, who seemed as embarrassed as he now was by their laughter.

Avis pulled the scarf from her head and obediently followed. Sierra took a few more whacks at her jeans and did the same. Valerie bent over and picked up a curved piece of metal from the ground. Ian rubbed the rust off his fingers onto the seat of his pants and wandered over next to her. He didn't know why, but he needed to say something.

"I didn't realize he'd messed with those springs."

"Well, no. I mean, who would have?"

Her hair had fallen forward when she'd bent over, and he very nearly reached out and tucked it back behind her ear. Instead, he stuffed his fingertips into his back pockets. Humor quivered at the corner of his mouth again. "I thought it might come apart, but criminy! It was like a grenade explosion, shrapnel ricocheting all over the place, pinging off…"

"Sheet metal," she finished for him, and as one they turned toward his truck.

"Ah, hell," Ian erupted, hurrying toward the gleaming vehicle. She was right beside him and together they went over the vulnerable side of the truck.

"Hmm, no, I don't see anything," she mumbled.

"Must've been the shed," he concluded in relief. "Or maybe the trailer. Better the trailer than the truck. I just bought this thing!"

"It's a nice one," she said, running a hand along the edge of the bed wall.

"I guess I'm kind of particular about my vehicles," he heard himself say for no particular reason.

She nodded. "I know what you mean. It's such a huge investment, isn't it? I nearly croaked when I saw the dent in my rear panel the other day."

"Aw, man, that stinks," he said, in perfect agreement with her.

"Never stops, though, does it?" she commented with a sigh. "It's one flipping catastrophe after another, and no money for any of them."

And just like that, it was over. The moment of mutual understanding, that odd, enveloping connection, gone. Anger sparked in her caramel-brown eyes, and his defenses rose straightaway to counter it.

"We all deal with that problem, Miss Blunt," he heard himself snap, "every damned one of us, and you know what? Money just doesn't matter much, not when you're talking life and death situations."

"Like springs coming apart and shooting through space?" she demanded hotly, flinging out an arm.

"What's your point?"

"That you can't always predict. You can take every precaution and disaster can still strike, or you can fail to recognize a potential catastrophe for years and years with absolutely no ramifications."

"You're going to move that hot water heater," he told her, somehow winding up with his finger wagging in her face. "It's dangerous."

"You could at least give me some time!" she argued.

"I've given you time!" he shouted, wanting to shake her. "Every day that you delay you're taking a chance with your life!"

She whipped away from him, striding rigidly toward the house. He watched the defiant sway of that neat little bottom and wanted to pull his hair out by the roots. What was wrong with the woman? Why couldn't she understand the danger? He shook his head, at a flat loss. The woman was nuts. That was the only explanation.

He had no explanation at all for why his gaze stayed glued to her petite form until she disappeared into the house or why regret twisted his insides. Maybe he was the nut. Heaven knew he didn't need some sexy little shrew eating at him, especially one who already had a boyfriend. He'd learned that much with a few casual questions around town.

Buddy Wilcox was a real piece of work, though. He was the laziest volunteer fireman on the Puma Springs force, and according to the word around town, the closest thing to a con man. Ian couldn't imagine what Valerie saw in the guy, but they apparently had a very long history together.

Despite her lousy taste in men, Ian couldn't deny how pleased he was that she and the other two had shown up to help Edwin. Maybe they realized how sick the old man was; he'd even thought, for a moment, that the women might know more, but he'd rejected that notion almost immediately. Edwin had demanded extreme discretion. His secrets were safe.

Ian told himself that he ought to forget about Valerie Blunt and ask out one of her attractive friends, but he knew he wasn't going to do that. It was best to concentrate on his job and put off establishing a social life just now. Those, after all, were things at which he was quite good.

"Ladies," Ian Keene said, mopping his brow with a crumpled bandanna as he looked around the neat yard, "you've been a tremendous help."

"Yup," Edwin agreed. "I hardly recognize the old place."

"Glad to do it," Avis said softly. Even grimy and exhausted, with her cheeks pinked from the sun, she looked feminine and pretty, a description Valerie knew that could not be applied to herself. She felt as if she'd been shaken in a bag of dirt and pulled through a keyhole backward.

"How about I buy you ladies a beer?" Ian offered affably.

"No," Val answered quickly. "We, uh, we have to get going." Maybe he wasn't a complete ogre, but she'd be hanged if she'd sit down to a beer with the man who had created such catastrophe in all their lives.

"Okay," Ian said lightly. "Another time maybe."

"That would be nice, thank you," Avis said, glancing in Valerie's direction.

"I do need to get home to my daughter," Sierra added apologetically.

Valerie frowned, then addressed herself to Edwin. "Well, I guess we'll be seeing you around."

"For a while yet," Edwin answered with a nod.

That seemed odd, but Val didn't have time to contemplate it as Ian Keene suddenly seemed eager to have them gone.

"Thanks again, ladies. Your willingness to help out here tells me that you'll each do all you must to bring your own places up to code."

Valerie rolled her eyes. Trust him to bring that up. She just couldn't win with this man! Sierra's and Avis's frowns told her that they agreed. Didn't they? They did not, as they made plain a few moments later when the three of them were walking along the recently cleared path toward the front gate.

The sun had sunk beyond the horizon some minutes earlier, and the slant of the waning light cast the overgrown pathway into deep shadow, so that Valerie could barely see Sierra at her elbow as she hissed, "In the future, you might consult Avis and me before you make a decision that concerns us."

Stung, Valerie snapped, "Surely you didn't want to have a beer with him?"

"Not looking like this," Avis admitted.

"But you could've at least consulted us," Sierra put in.

"Well, excuse me," Valerie retorted defensively, "but since we came together in *my* car I naturally assumed we'd be leaving together."

"You just can't admit you were wrong about him," Avis stated softly.

"Face it, Val," Sierra said. "He's not the villain we thought he was."

Valerie's jaw dropped. "Do you hear yourselves? He's responsible for all our troubles. We've worked our fingers to the bone here today because *he* threatened to prosecute poor Edwin.''

''For heaven's sake, Val,'' Avis insisted, ''the man is just doing his job.''

''This place was dangerous. Surely you could see that,'' Sierra agreed.

''Oh, and I suppose our places are dangerous, too,'' she scoffed.

''I suspect they are.'' Avis sighed. ''Mine is, anyway. I'm always blowing fuses and overheating extension cords. Suppose if we asked him he'd help us get our places up to code?''

Sierra clucked her tongue, considering. ''Looks like he's got more than enough to do already.''

''Yeah. He's got to hurry around town causing problems for people minding their own business.'' Valerie threw up her hands. ''Just because the man looks good enough to eat and picks up some trash doesn't mean that he's a nice guy!''

Sierra and Avis just glanced at one another and burst out laughing.

''What?'' Valerie demanded, truly puzzled. ''It's not funny. The man has acquired a little bit of power, and it's obviously gone to his head. If you can't see that, then I guess it's up to me to bring him down a peg.''

Sierra folded her arms, nodding sagely. ''I guess it is, Val.''

''Yes, I'd say you're definitely the woman for that job,'' Avis agreed.

For the life of her, Valerie couldn't figure out what

that meant. Nose aloft, she swept between them, saying, "Fine. Just see if I don't."

Everything in her screamed that Ian Keene was not just the handsome new fire marshal going routinely about his job. Something in her *recognized* something in him, something worrisome, something slightly dangerous. She shivered just thinking about the almost predatory look that had come into those bright blue eyes of his during the moments they'd remained in the yard alone. No matter what everyone else seemed to think, she knew that Ian Keene was a threat. She'd have staked her life on it.

Valerie stood staring at the two notices, one in each hand, with a sense of deep dismay and imminent failure. The failure was rightly Dillon's. The Monday afternoon post had brought another letter from his university. He had failed a second class! Hundreds of dollars worth of tuition and fees had been paid out for nothing, and as if to underscore the fact that she kept putting out her hard-earned money for no good reason at all, Ian Keene's Office of the Fire Marshal had officially notified her that her shop was in non-compliance with established city code, and that would be twenty-five dollars, thank you very much, for an unwanted inspection and a world full of trouble.

Twenty-five dollars! He expected her to pay him twenty-five dollars for turning her life upside down? It was beyond belief.

She could do nothing about Dillon's mess, but Ian Keene was another thing. She snatched up her purse, then hung a "Back in 15 Minutes" sign in the door window and flew out of the shop.

Ian tidied the growing stack of papers in his out-box and reached for his coffee cup. He was making good progress, but the paperwork that came with the job was a never-ending barrage of local, state and federal forms. Though his least favorite part of the position, it came with the territory, and he'd studied the ever-changing mountain of regulations in preparation for this career move. He had a plan, and this tiny, utilitarian office in a three-bay fire station, the only one in town, was just the first step in that plan.

He was still a stranger to Puma Springs in many ways, but a kind of ownership was growing on him. This was his town, and it definitely needed cleaning up. He looked forward to the day when he didn't cringe with unnecessary worry every time he drove around town. For now, he was devoting three days a week to inspections and the other two to paperwork. Brent Hawley, his assistant and a good friend and firefighter, pulled the night shift and spent his time keeping the pumper, ladder truck, ambulance and other gear in good order.

Ian had hired Brent because the burly, freckle-faced redhead had expressed a blunt desire to placate his pregnant wife by minimizing his risks in the line of duty. Ian understood the motive. He was the first to admit that if he'd been willing to do the same thing his own short marriage might have survived beyond its first anniversary. He hadn't been willing, and Mary Beth had walked away. He didn't blame her.

Setting aside his cup, Ian reached for the next form. Cato suddenly hauled up to all fours and whined excitedly. The next instant, the door to Ian's office opened and Valerie Blunt stalked in. She slapped a piece of paper onto his desk blotter, then staggered sideways as Cato reared up and tried to wrap his forelegs around her waist. For some reason that crazy dog of his adored this woman.

Actually, Cato was anything but crazy, and Valerie Blunt was pretty adorable with her artfully shaggy hair swinging about her chin and her golden eyes flashing fire at him. As she shoved the dog away, he picked up the paper.

"As if you don't know what it says," she sneered.

His eyebrows lifted. "It says someone named Dillon Blunt has failed Advanced Economics."

She gasped, grabbed the paper, then stuffed it into her coat pocket. "That's not the one. I meant to bring the other one."

"What other one?"

"You know perfectly well!" she snapped, planting her hands on the front edge of his desk and leaning forward. The deep V of the yellow-gold top she wore beneath a loose, blue cotton coat gaped invitingly. He sat forward in his chair, folded his arms against the blotter and looked straight down her blouse. It was not a wise move. One glimpse of the firm mounds of her pale golden breasts and the deep cleft between them and his jeans were strangling him.

"Twenty-five dollars!" she accused. "It just never stops with you, does it?"

Ah. He bullied his gaze upward. It locked on her

mouth. She wore bronze lipstick today, darker than usual. He swallowed, gathered his scattered thoughts and croaked out, "Not my doing. The city council—"

"The city council didn't storm into my shop, dictate that I have to spend hundreds of dollars, then charge me twenty-five bucks for the privilege!"

"They decided on the twenty-five dollar charge after I did your inspection."

"I don't care! I won't pay it!" she cried.

Something she'd said before clicked into place. Hundreds of dollars to have a plumber's mistake resolved? Uh-uh. Not on his watch, not for a violation that the plumber should have known about from the beginning.

"I take it you've spoken to the plumber. This would be the same plumber who installed the hot water heater?"

"Yes, of course."

He picked up an ink pen, saying, "I'll be needing his name."

She didn't answer immediately. Instead, she hitched a leg up onto the corner of his desk, perching there with her weight levered onto one thigh. He couldn't help noticing that her little flowered skirt left a whole lot of leg showing, more leg than a woman who barely reached his shoulder ought to possess.

"Look, I know you take your job very seriously, but I don't want to get anybody else into trouble."

"That plumber should be fully informed about the city code before he makes another mistake, don't you think?"

She leapt off his desk. "It's four little inches! Can't we just forget it?"

"Proper ventilation is essential to a gas water heater," he said, injecting authority into his voice. "Otherwise, you run the risk of carbon monoxide poisoning. It's colorless, tasteless, odorless, and deadly, and I suspect that the only reason you haven't felt its effects already is because the door is opening and closing all the time at your shop, letting in fresh air. But what happens when the weather gets warm or cold and your air unit is constantly recirculating the air? If you're lucky you'll get nauseous and sleepy and develop a skull-splitter of a headache. If you're not, the thing will simply explode. Mark my words, Valerie, unless that water heater's moved so that it's properly ventilated, someone's going to get hurt."

She gulped and frowned. "That doesn't make it fair. Especially not the twenty-five dollars."

He didn't much like that part of it himself, but the city had to offset costs somehow. "Twenty-five bucks doesn't even cover the paperwork involved."

The dog jumped up on her again, planting his massive paws on her shoulders and wagging his tongue in her face. She held it off by ruffling its ears.

"I shelled out over nine hundred dollars to have that darned water heater replaced," she grumbled.

He poised the pen over a scrap of paper. "I want the plumber's name."

"Duane Compton," she muttered, and Cato took advantage of her momentary lack of vigilance to thoroughly lick her face. She laughed, and the sound of it did strange things to Ian's stomach.

"Cato, get down," he ordered, unable to control his own smile.

The dog obediently dropped to the floor, whining imploringly. Valerie rolled her eyes and followed him down, crouching on the floor in front of Ian's desk. "I ought to be mad at you, too," she told the dog, scratching under the heavy black chin. Cato flopped over, wriggling in delight. "You got me into this," she complained, rubbing down the animal's torso, "you and that nose of yours."

Ian sat forward, grinning at the way the dog's tongue lolled out the side of his mouth. He was in doggy heaven, the lucky mutt. "He likes you."

She looked up ruefully. "So I've noticed."

"You should be flattered. He's quite the hero, you know. He saved his original owner, an elderly man, from a fire. Woke him in the middle of the night."

"How did you come to have him?"

"The old guy fell and broke a hip. His family decided he should go to a nursing home, so he asked me to take Cato. That was almost four years ago, and I've never seen this mutt as nuts about anybody as he is about you."

"Must be my perfume or something," she mumbled.

"Something," he said. His own list of attractions went quite a bit further than perfume at the moment. She was downright intriguing when she wasn't spitting fire—*and* when she was. He watched her small, coral-tipped hands stroke the dog and found it a little difficult to breathe properly. He noticed the delicate bones of her wrists and ankles, the curvy roundness of her hip and thigh as she crouched there petting his dog. She would fit very neatly in his lap. "Listen, about that twenty-five bucks," he said. "I'll see what I can do about it, okay?"

She stiffened at the mere mention of the fee and pushed up to her feet. He realized too late that he'd just reminded her of their conflict.

"I'd say that's the least you could do," she told him haughtily. With that she swept out of the office, slamming the door behind her.

Cato got up, whining pathetically.

"Give it up, pal," Ian muttered, shaking his head even as he reached for a telephone book and flipped it open. "She's obviously not for us, so we both might as well quit drooling over her."

Cato swung his big head around. The look in his black eyes seemed to say, *"Easier said than done, boss."* Silently agreeing, Ian looked up the plumber's number and made the call.

Chapter Four

Valerie watched the plumber measure a length of small pipe. "I appreciate you cutting your price, Mr. Compton, but I'm short of cash at the moment. I'll have to pay this out over time."

The small, reed thin man gave her a disgruntled look, but she couldn't do anything about his displeasure.

The front door opened, and she hurried from the back room to the front of the shop, hoping for a drop-in customer. Ian Keene greeted her.

"I take it Compton is here?"

"Yes, in time to beat your arbitrary deadline," she answered huffily.

"It isn't arbitrary," he said, moving toward her. "It's mandatory. I could've shut you down, you know, and if the weather wasn't so mild, I would have.''

That surprised her, but she quickly buried a spurt of gratitude beneath stubborn resentment. Twisting his shoulders, he brushed past her. She followed him into the back room. The plumber got up off his knees as Ian bore down on him.

''Marshal Keene.'' The poor man seemed to shrink, looking positively diminutive next to Ian's tall, broad-shouldered form. ''What're you doing here?''

''I dropped by to inspect your work.''

The plumber's eyes darted side to side. ''A-ain't finished yet.''

''That's all right. I'll just watch.''

Duane Compton frowned with obvious disgust, then he looked to Valerie, who offered him an understanding smile. At last, someone who didn't like Ian Keene any better than she did.

Compton rocked side to side nervously and blurted, ''Been thinking it over and decided not to charge you for moving this here heater.''

Dumbfounded, Valerie watched as Ian smugly parked his hands at his waist.

''Since you're being fair about this,'' he said, ''I'll see to it that you're not fined for ignoring established code. This time.''

Relief began to flow through Val as it dawned on her that she wasn't going to be out all that money. Understanding followed. If Ian hadn't shown up here today, Compton would have charged her anyway, with no one the wiser! She felt dizzy as her assumptions and biases tilted. After all the ugly things she'd thought and said, Ian Keene had cut her a break! She ducked her head to hide the stain of color that rose to her cheeks.

"I—I think I can manage the inspection fee now," she offered timidly, darting a glance upward.

Ian just waved that away. "Taken care of." He glared at the plumber, who quickly went back to work. Valerie glared at him as well, finally realizing who the unscrupulous character in this little drama really was. Humbled, Valerie swallowed down the last of her pride and looked to Ian.

"He was going to charge me half price on his estimate before you got here."

Ian moved to her side and, taking her by the arm, ushered her a little farther down the long, narrow room, his hand burning right through the sleeves of her smock and blouse. "I thought he might try something like that. He struck me as the sort to take advantage of a pretty young woman."

Valerie's eyes flew wide and her jaw dropped. "You think I'm pretty?"

Ian looked as surprised as she felt. "Of course I do."

She collapsed back against the wall in a mild state of shock. "Oh, my gosh, was that a compliment?"

He frowned. "You know you're pretty."

"I know *you* think so," she said cheekily, flirting madly.

He smiled, leaned his face close to hers and said softly, "You may not be the most beautiful woman I've ever seen, but you're damned sure the most *attractive*."

The thrill that shot through her brought an intense awareness. Suddenly virile, masculine power oozed from every pore of his body. She sensed the weight of his bones and muscle, the firmness of his skin, the strength in his broad, long-fingered hands. He smiled lazily, as if aware of her every thought, of every sensation, every emanation that touched her, and she smiled back, agog with the potency of the attraction that had suddenly sprung to life between them. Then a crackle of electricity rent the air, followed by a tinny, urgent voice.

"Fire One, this is Dispatch. Fire One can you hear me?"

Ian quickly straightened and dragged up a small radio tethered to his belt. Holding it close to his mouth, he depressed a button and spoke. "What's up?"

"We just got a 911. It's Edwin Searle. I've dispatched the ambulance, but I knew you'd want to go."

Edwin! Valerie suddenly remembered, inanely, that it was Thursday.

"Damn!" For an instant, Ian's gaze met hers with a look so loaded that it fairly shouted of special knowledge. Then he was on his way out the door.

Valerie stood frozen for a second longer, then her feet were suddenly moving. "I'll be back!" she shouted at the plumber. She was running by the time she hit the sidewalk. "Wait!" she screamed at Ian as he opened the door of his truck. "Wait!" She reached the coffee shop in three long strides and wrenched open the door, yelling, "Something's happened to Edwin!"

Gwyn stuck her head out of the kitchen. "What?"

"Edwin Searle! Tell the others!"

Gwyn nodded and hurried forward. Valerie was already leaping off the raised walk. Ian's truck lurched forward with a screech of tires and swung left, coming to a halt just as she reached it. Valerie jerked open the door and jumped in.

"Hurry," she begged as Ian flipped on the emergency lights mounted atop the cab and barked, "Belt up!"

She fumbled for her safety belt and started to pray.

Ian hit the siren and gunned the engine through a red light. Beside him, Valerie beat a small fist against her knee. He knew he shouldn't have let her come along. They would probably beat the local ambulance. Slowing the truck slightly, Ian whipped a right turn and depressed the gas pedal to make up speed. Val jerked and swayed but didn't complain.

"What do you think it is?" she asked worriedly.

Ian considered not answering, then heard himself grimly say, "His heart. Edwin's been in the last stages of congestive heart failure for weeks."

Before he could say more, they were there. He brought the truck to a dusty stop beside the open gate and jumped out. He could hear voices, low voices, and knew in his gut that it was too late. He turned just in time to catch Valerie as she barreled up behind him, his arms clasped firmly about her waist. She looked up at him and seemed to understand that the need to rush was purely emotional. Together they walked around the old pecan tree. Half a dozen people milled about the yard. Edwin lay stretched out on his back, hands at his sides, face turned up to the sky, jaw set. His cowboy hat had been placed on his chest.

Valerie broke into a run and dropped to her knees beside him. Ian followed, going down at her side as he reached with two fingers to try to locate a pulse in the folds of Edwin's neck. He found none. Val began to weep quietly. Ian pulled up a knee and rested his forearm across it, swallowing down the lump in his throat. In the distance he could hear the wail of the ambulance siren. Looking up, he asked, ''Who found him?''

A grizzled, middle-aged man in coveralls and a billed cap, cleared his throat.

''I did. Saw him out walking yesterday evening. Didn't think he looked too good. He said he was having some trouble with his circulation and thought some exercise might help, but I noticed that he was short of breath, so I figured I better check on him this morning. Found him here in the yard, on his side.'' He pointed at a stout, mid-thirtyish woman and said, ''Miz Mooney, she's a nurse. Lives up the road a bit. I went straightaway to her, and we called 911 from there.''

The woman had tried CPR, but Ian knew it had been too late even then. He thanked them both for their efforts.

Valerie lifted her tear-wet face to the man, asking brokenly, ''You don't suppose he's been here all this time, do you?''

"Since yesterday evening? No, ma'am. He's wearing different clothes this morning, clean-shaven. I think it must've happened not long before I found him."

"It's Thursday," she whispered. "He'd have wanted his haircut and flowers." She looked at Ian and said, "He's with her now. They're together again."

Ian folded her tight against his side. The siren had grown louder and tires sounded on gravel. The ambulance had arrived.

Someone said, "Guess the mayor ought to know."

Valerie stiffened slightly. Ian nodded, but no one moved off to make the call. For several seconds, they waited in silence, then a metallic jingle and faint rumble alerted them to the arrival of the gurney. Ian pulled her up to her feet and moved her back out of the way, keeping his arms tight about her. As two of the volunteer EMT crew, one a night clerk at the convenience store and the other a local pastor, lifted the body onto the stretcher, Val began to sob softly again.

"I think he was ready for this," Ian told her. "He knew his time was limited."

They watched as the minister carefully arranged the hands, then gently pulled up the sides of the body bag that had been folded and opened on top of the stretcher. Ian had liked Edwin, understood him. They were both loners, each in his own way. Yet Edwin had found someone. Ian looked down into Val's tear-washed eyes, and something twisted inside him.

They followed, arm in arm, as the gurney slowly bumped over the ground. They heard another vehicle pulling up, and then they stepped through the gate and saw that Sierra and Avis had arrived in Sierra's battered old flower shop van.

"What's happened?" Avis gasped as she ran toward Valerie. Sierra joined her, the tears already rolling down her face.

"Oh, my God, he's dead, isn't he?"

"They think it was his heart," Valerie said tearfully, pulling away from Ian to go to her friends. The three of them huddled there, hugging and weeping.

Ian watched them, thinking that this was right, as it should be. The three of them had no inkling what was coming, and that was as it should be, too. He looked at Valerie and understood how her life would change. He could only wonder if he would have any part in it at all.

The mourners arrayed themselves around the bier supporting the simple black steel casket. A green grass carpet hid the yawning pit carved into the rocky dirt. Edwin's pastor stood next to the headstone. Heston and his mousy wife, the only actual family members present, sat in folding chairs beneath a green awning. Valerie, Avis and Sierra stood together with Ian directly behind them in a navy-blue dress uniform, a flat service cap with a patent-leather bill, white shirt and ice-blue tie that made his eyes shine like bits of sky captured in glass. On the opposite side of the casket huddled a cluster of Edwin's peers, seeing off another of their own.

Valerie listened to the sound of the minister's voice rather than his words. She'd been in a fugue these past two days. The loss had touched her on a personal level that she hadn't felt since the death of her father. She held hands with Sierra and Avis, comforted that they, too, mourned Edwin's passing.

The minister intoned a prayer, and then it was over. Heston and the wife were halfway to the car before the true mourners had so much as lifted their heads. Valerie, Sierra and Avis traded disgusted looks before starting back to the car. Ian strode alone to his truck and waved to them before sliding behind the wheel.

The women piled silently into Val's dented car and drove back to the strip mall, where they first went, by mutual agreement, to the coffee shop. Gwyn had refused to attend the funeral, saying that Edwin wouldn't have expected or particularly wanted her there. Valerie suspected that she had merely wanted to avoid making an emotional display. Ian walked in a few minutes later, wearing his usual jeans and sport shirt, and calmly moved a chair to the end of their table.

"I figured this would be the place to be," he commented, sitting down. "Our esteemed mayor certainly wasn't about to open his home for a reception."

"You can say that again," Sierra muttered.

"Do you ever wonder," Avis asked, "how different Edwin might have been if he hadn't lost Marge?"

"Of if he hadn't met her," Ian put in.

They all pondered that for a moment, then Valerie said, "I think it's terribly sweet and terribly sad how he missed her."

"It was no reason to be surly," Gwyn said flatly, returning to plunk a water glass down in front of Ian.

"Everyone loses something or someone. That's life." She looked down at Ian. "Want anything else?"

He smiled up at her. "A piece of that famous peach pie wouldn't go amiss."

Gwyn turned away, opining, "And I suppose you want it heated with cream." She took the pie into the back, where she would slice it and warm a piece in the microwave before pouring cream around the edges of the bowl.

Ian grinned. "She sure works at being tough."

"I don't suppose it's any of our business," Avis said, "but something's there, some reason for all that toughness."

"Usually is," Ian remarked.

Gwyn returned with the hot pie before hurrying off. She nodded at the window and said, "Avis, isn't that a customer of yours pulling up?"

Avis stretched upward to look over Sierra's head. "Yes. Thank you." She quickly gathered her handbag. "Sorry. Duty calls."

"I'd better get back to business, too," Sierra said, getting to her feet as Avis darted out the door. "Those bills don't pay themselves."

"Don't worry about it," Ian said. "It'll change for the better soon."

"One can hope," Sierra returned doubtfully, moving away.

"You're not hurrying off, too, are you?" Ian asked Val, picking up his spoon.

She shrugged. "I canceled all my appointments for this afternoon, *both* of them."

Ian chuckled and dived into the pie. After several

bites, he dabbed his mouth with a thin paper napkin. "How're you doing?"

She sighed. "Okay. This has kind of thrown me back to when my dad died. Car wreck. I was sixteen."

Ian winced. "Tough age. You were close, weren't you?"

She smiled at that. "Yeah. We were close. You know how it is."

He nodded. "I have a sister. My brother and I watched her wrap Dad around her pinky for years and years." He grinned. "I figured you for that sort, frankly."

She laughed. "Tell me about your family."

He shrugged. "Well, I'm the oldest. I have a sister and a brother. Lois is thirty-two, married, two kids. She's a nurse, lives in Lubbock. My folks moved out there after Mom had her stroke so Sis could help out. Mom's pretty much recovered, but they seem content in West Texas."

"And your brother?"

"Warren's a cop in Fort Worth."

"Do you see him much?"

He looked down. "Not lately. This job keeps me pretty busy."

"But you worry about him, don't you?"

"Hell, yes." He lifted a hand. "Don't say it. I know that fighting fire is dangerous, but Warren has a family depending on him. He's got a wife and four-year-old daughter."

"So you think he should quit the force?"

"Maybe."

"I understand. I have a brother of my own."

"Ah yes, Dillon. The scholar."

She snorted. "And he's failing another class," she said. "I've practically killed myself to keep him in school, and he can't even be bothered to go to class."

"Maybe you should cut him loose," Ian suggested mildly.

"Is that what you would do?"

He turned a sheepish look up at her. "Probably not. I'd probably kick his butt and tighten the thumb screws until he buckled down."

"Works for me. Unfortunately I don't quite have the brawn to pull that off."

"Well, buck up," he said. "Things are going to change soon."

"You think?"

"They always do, don't they?"

"Usually for the worse," she told him.

"Not this time."

"What makes you say so?"

He dropped his gaze again. "Well, since you don't seem to think I'm here just to make your life miserable and drain your bank account any longer, I figure anything can happen."

She laughed. "You might be right."

He cleared his throat and looked up again, blue gaze measuring. "I've heard you're seeing Buddy Wilcox."

She snorted at that. "I wish. I'd like to see him pay for the dent he put in my car, and then I'd like to see him disappear into thin air. Permanently."

Ian smiled cautiously. "Are you saying that the two of you aren't a couple?"

"Does it matter?"

"Yeah. It matters."

Valerie caught her breath. "We're not a couple. I'm not seeing anyone."

He lifted his gaze to hers. "Maybe you ought to start."

Valerie coyly dropped her gaze, her heart beating fast. "Ian Keene, are you trying to ask me out on a date?"

"Would you go if I was?"

"Absolutely."

Those dangerous blue eyes crinkled attractively at the outside edges. "I was thinking dinner. Soon. Real soon."

A smile rolled across her face. It seemed her luck *was* changing for the better, after all.

Chapter Five

Ian aimed the key toward the lock in the driver's side door of the truck only to drop the ring before reaching his target. Bending quickly, he snatched them up, silently scolding himself. It was a simple date, for pity's sake, not a burning orphanage. He needed to get a grip. The fact that the woman now belting herself into the passenger seat of his pickup looked as edible as cherry pie and twice as tasty was not an adequate excuse for the case of nerves that he'd been fighting all afternoon. He'd polished his boots twice before he'd even realized what he was doing! It hadn't helped to see her standing there looking like dessert. That shiny, tomato-red lipstick in the exact same shade as her short, form-fitting little dress had turned him into a bumbling clod.

Taking a deep breath, he calmly opened the truck

door and slid up into his seat. "The steak house okay with you? We could always drive into Fort Worth."

"Why bother? Local food and margaritas would be good." She fixed a bright smile on her face, and he nearly swallowed his tongue. What was it about her?

He managed to get them, without further incident, to the shabby-chic steak house a block from downtown. It was a family place, a sort of PG version of a supper club. The bartender, who kept a watchful eye on the door, greeted them the instant they walked in. "Hey, Marshal, Val."

"Hey, Skeet!" Valerie called brightly. "We'll take the table by the window."

"Suit yourself. I'll send Liz over in a minute."

"Skeet?" Ian asked softly as they walked toward the table she'd pointed out. "I thought his name was Robert."

"Old nickname. We went to school together." She grinned as he pulled out her chair and parked her sweet behind on the wood seat.

He took the chair opposite her. "Should I guess what your nickname was?"

"Didn't have one for some reason."

"Uh-oh. That means you either flew below the radar or were very, very popular." He shook his head. "Definitely not below the radar. So who am I taking out here," he teased, "the head cheerleader?"

"Not the *head* cheerleader," she said, grinning impishly, "but I was the homecoming queen."

"Ooh. I finally hit the big time."

She laughed. "What about you? No, let me guess. Football team."

He shook his head. "Uh-uh. I fancied a career in rodeo back then. Rode all the junior events I could get to."

"What made you give it up?"

"Just didn't have what it takes," he admitted easily. "Too big for bull riding, not enough finesse for calf roping."

"What about the other big-man sports like steer wrestling and saddle bronc?"

"Didn't seem glamorous enough at the time. So you know rodeo?"

She shrugged. "This is Texas, isn't it? My dad used to dabble. Saddle bronc. Mom hated it. She was afraid he'd get himself killed." She looked down at her hands and said softly, "He wasn't known for his caution."

The waitress, a middle-aged woman sporting a steel-gray ponytail, arrived with water glasses, chips and salsa. "So," she said, "two rib eyes?"

The rib eye was the specialty of the house, and Ian had to admit that he'd seldom had better. "Sounds good to me."

"Me, too," Valerie agreed brightly.

"How do you want them?"

"Medium," they said in unison, then touched gazes and smiled.

"Spuds?"

"Baked," they said together, eyebrows lifting, gazes holding.

"Loaded?" the waitress asked, unimpressed.

"No cheese," Ian said.

At the same instant Valerie said, "Hold the

cheese.'' She looked at him, and they both burst out laughing.

The waitress didn't seem to notice. ''Salad dressing?''

Ian waved a hand at Valerie. ''Honey mustard,'' she said.

He made a face and told the waitress, ''Ranch.''

''And what are we drinking?''

''Beer for me,'' Ian said.

Val made a face this time. ''Margarita.''

The waitress turned away. ''Be right out.''

''Let's see,'' Ian said, ''three out of five. We're practically compatible.''

''Close enough.''

Ian smiled. This was a Valerie he hadn't seen before, happy-go-lucky, fun. His thoughts drifted to what this new Valerie would be like in bed, though he tried to warn himself to go slow. He loaded a chip with salsa but dropped it as trouble walked up.

''Hey, baby,'' Buddy Wilcox said, draping his arm around Valerie's chair and bending to drop a kiss on her face. She jerked and turned her head at the last instant, pushing him away.

''What do think you're doing, Buddy?''

He glanced at Ian. ''Talking to my girl.''

''Your girl?'' Valerie scoffed. ''In a pig's eye, and I'm looking at the pig.''

''Aw, come on, don't be like that,'' Buddy said, reaching out a hand to flick at her bare shoulder. Ian gritted his teeth, but Valerie was very much in control here.

"Don't be like what, Buddy? Like I don't know what a loser you are?"

Buddy's face hardened. "So you say, but you keep coming back, don't you?"

"No. Not for a long time."

He raised his voice. "Everyone knows you're my girl."

She smirked. "Buddy, you and I haven't been on an actual date in months, not that I'd expect you to notice."

"We've been busy," he defended petulantly.

"I've been busy *and* uninterested," she corrected. "You've been lying around on your butt seeing how much beer you can soak up. By the way, you owe me seven hundred and fifty bucks for the dent you put in my car."

He grinned, trying to charm her. "That's what insurance is for, sugar."

"You are screwed in the head if you think I'm going to bump up my rates by making a claim for something you did."

"You really shouldn't say things you don't mean."

"True. Now, get lost, Buddy, and I do mean it."

"Maybe I don't want to."

"Maybe you'd like some help," Ian said through his teeth.

Buddy sent him a venomous look, but it was wary, too. Already slinking away, he glanced at Val. "We'll continue this later."

"Years later," Val retorted. "Obnoxious, overgrown boy." She shook her head, then smiled and said, "It's nice to deal with a real man for a change."

Pleased and encouraged, Ian reached across the table and covered her hand with his, thinking that he'd like to show her just how *manly* he was feeling.

Valerie bounced up the stairs toward her apartment, delight and pure lust percolating inside her. "Wow," she said, feeling oddly dizzy, "Skeet must've mixed the drinks a little strong tonight."

Ian's big, heavy hand slid beneath her arm from the back, cupping the dip of her waist and steadying her. "I don't think it's the alcohol. You only had two."

She reached the landing and turned, arms flung out with uncontainable exultation. "Then just what is it, Mr. Fire Marshal Gorgeous Keene?"

He stopped on the second step down, a lazy smile on his face, promise in the electric depths of those blue eyes. "Gorgeous, did you say? I think you better invite me in so we can discuss that."

"I don't think so," she said, feeling reckless as she dug her keys from her small handbag. She crossed to the door, unlocked it and shoved the door wide, stepping back to allow him entrance. "Discuss, that is."

He slowly climbed the last two steps, walked across the landing and stepped into her apartment, holding her gaze all the way. She followed, closed the door and reached for the light switch in the tiny entry, but his hand covered hers, and she felt herself turned, lifted slightly and pulled against him.

His mouth found hers unerringly in the dark. She dropped purse and keys and wrapped her arms around him. The kiss was everything she had imagined it would be. When he drove his tongue into her mouth, she went up on tiptoe, plastering herself against him. He was big and hard and hot, his mouth mobile and expert. Her body tightened and flooded. He dropped his hands to her bottom, yanking her upward and completely off her feet. She wrapped her legs around him, bringing their bodies into perfect symmetry.

He put his head back, holding her there, open to him, and gasped, "I've wanted to do that all night. Your lipstick's been driving me crazy. It suits you. Red suits you. I'm beginning to think everything about you suits me."

She pulled his head down to hers once more, not daring to think where this was leading, what the result could be. This was uncharted territory for her, but even the perils looked attractive just then. She didn't care that she'd thought him the source of all her woes only days ago, that she never, ever did this sort of thing, that she could regret it all shortly. He turned and took one long step forward, pinning her against the wall there with his body and urgent mouth.

While his tongue thrust repeatedly into the sensitive depths of her mouth, his hands slid over her, skimming her bottom, legs, arms, breasts, the creases in her thighs where they met her hips. She thought wildly of tearing his shirt off, running her hands over his bare skin.

A dim crackle pecked at her attention, but it was easy to ignore. Even when the voice came, she just couldn't quite pay heed to it, though the words did register.

"Fire One, this is Fire Two on report."

Ian pushed against the juncture of her thighs, groaning.

"Fire One? Fire One, this is Fire Two."

She understood then. It was the radio that he wore clipped to his belt. Ian made a sound of frustration and broke the kiss, his big hands splayed across her rib cage just beneath her breasts. He pressed his forehead to hers.

"Ian? Are you there? Are you all right?"

He reached down for the thing, jerking it upward with a muffled curse. Valerie put her head back and sucked in enough air to begin clearing her mind.

"Yeah?" Ian barked into the radio. "What is it?"

"You okay?" the voice in the radio wanted to know.

Valerie began to realize how exposed she was in this position and, pushing gently at his shoulders, lowered her legs. With a sigh, Ian laid his forehead against the wall and allowed her to slide down to her feet. Finally, he backed up a step and spoke into the radio again. "Brent, this had better be very important."

"Ladder's out of commission."

Ian lifted a hand to the back of his neck. "What now?" he said into the radio.

"Radiator hose. Someone has to drive into Fort Worth and find a twenty-four-hour parts store."

Ian sighed richly. "Yeah, yeah. On my way. Out." He clipped the radio to his belt. "This thing has become the bane of my existence, but I have to respond to this. The ladder truck can't be down. Maybe I could drop by later?"

She squared her shoulders and sucked in a deep breath. She wasn't the sort to lose her head over a guy, but that was just what had been happening here. Not wise. "I think maybe we were getting ahead of ourselves," she said firmly.

For a moment he said nothing, then, "Well, it felt damned good on this end."

She smiled. "This one, too. Still, we were getting ahead of ourselves."

"Okay. If you say so." He grimaced.

She stepped to the door and opened it. Light flooded the tiny vestibule. "Anyway, you better get out of here. Sounds like you've got a situation working."

He nodded, crooked a finger beneath her chin and dropped a leisurely kiss on her mouth. "Good night." He walked out onto the landing.

"Ian," she suddenly called.

He turned. "Yeah?"

"Thank you. I don't mean for dinner. Well, I do, but mostly I mean… I've been going through a pretty rough patch financially, and I blamed you for making things worse when you were just doing your job. I wanted someone to blame, I guess, so thank you for not holding it against me."

For a moment he just looked at her. Then he admitted, "I should have told you up front that the installer was liable. I just…you bugged me, okay? Took me a while to figure out why. You're not the type I'm usually attracted to, frankly."

She folded her arms, prepared not to like what was coming next. "Why not?"

A hand drifted up to the back of his neck. "I don't know. I mean, I thought I had it figured out, what appeals to me about a woman and what doesn't, but you turn it all upside down somehow."

"Is that good?"

"I'm not sure," he answered honestly. "I just know I want to see you again."

"I'd like that," she told him softly, and after a moment, he nodded, turned and went on his way.

Valerie checked her watch and went back to combing out the steel-blue bouffant of the elderly woman in her chair. She had a cut-and-blow waiting, then it was time for her afternoon break with the girls. Today, of all days, she wanted that afternoon confab. All day yesterday, during church and the afternoon spent with her mother, she'd kept the news of her budding relationship with Ian Keene to herself, but the need to talk about it was growing exponentially as time passed. She really needed some input, and Avis, Sierra and Gwyn were the only ones she trusted to give her clear-eyed advice without the temptation to gossip.

Val was up to her elbows in lather when the postman appeared, form and pen in hand, expecting her to sign for a registered letter. She tried to put him off, worrying that it would be bad news, a dun, perhaps. He was insistent, however, and she finally relented, leaving the letter in the pocket of her smock as she continued with the job at hand. Twenty minutes later she breezed into the coffee shop, only to be drawn up short when Sierra twisted in her chair, an unfolded sheet of paper in her hand and asked, "Did you get a registered letter, too?"

She had managed to put the thing out of mind but dug it out of her pocket now. "As a matter of fact, I did. Haven't read it yet."

"Well, you'd better," Sierra advised. "It's from Edwin's attorney."

"Edwin?" Puzzled and curious, Val ripped open the letter and extracted the single sheet of paper. Unfolding it, she scanned the words written there with growing amazement. Her presence was required at the reading of the final will and testament of one Edwin Hale Searle, deceased, on Thursday of that very week, ten o'clock in the morning, at the attorney's office in downtown Puma Springs.

"What on earth?"

"That's what we've been trying to figure out," Sierra said.

"I can't believe he mentioned the three of us in his will," Avis commented. "I wonder who else is involved?"

"Well, Heston, most likely," Gwyn said.

"Oh, my God, he wouldn't have left us the ranch, would he?" Valerie suddenly thought aloud.

Gwyn waved a hand in dismissal of that notion. "Oh, it's some keepsakes he put back for each of you," she insisted.

"It can't be much," Valerie surmised, "considering the way he lived."

"I wouldn't mind having something to remember him by, though," Sierra said.

"Still, it's darn strange for you three to be mentioned in the will,'' Gwyn muttered, ''especially when you know he didn't have anything much to leave.''

''Except the ranch,'' Avis said worriedly.

The three of them looked at each other, and Sierra shook her head. ''Naw. He told me once that was tied up in some sort of family trust.''

They sat there, pondering the possibilities, then Val shrugged. ''No use speculating, I guess.''

''We'll find out Thursday,'' Avis said. ''Hey, you don't suppose Ian Keene got one of these, too, do you?''

''I don't know,'' Valerie answered, ''but I'll ask when he calls me.'' A new interest came to light in three pairs of feminine eyes. Valerie smiled slyly. ''We went out to dinner Saturday night.''

''I knew it,'' Avis announced, elbowing Sierra. ''Didn't I tell you?''

''No! Really?'' Valerie exclaimed. ''Well. Considering how I blamed him for everything, I have to say I'm surprised. And kind of confused, frankly.''

''Why so?'' Sierra prodded.

Valerie spread her hands. ''He bluntly admitted that he can't figure out why he's attracted to me.''

Avis and Sierra traded looks. ''Hmm,'' Avis murmured. ''That could be very, very good or very, very bad.''

''Meaning?''

''Meaning that it could be a case of opposites attracting,'' Sierra said, ''or—''

''A guy with one thing in mind,'' Gwyn put in, ''and once he gets it, it's, 'Sorry, babe, it's not going to work out, after all.'''

Valerie gulped as Avis reached across the table and patted her hand. "Just take it slow, hon. It'll work out."

"One way or the other," Gwyn cracked. "Usually the other."

"Oh, I don't know," Sierra said. "Ian seems like a really nice guy. I don't think he'd lead you down the garden path on purpose."

"Still, sensible is best," Avis counseled. "Give it time. Just give it time."

"When he calls you again, just explain that you want to take it slow," Sierra advised.

"*If* he calls you again," Gwyn said.

"Oh, he'll call," Val told them confidently, remembering that last gaspingly hot kiss. "I know he'll call."

Chapter Six

Ian didn't call. Not Monday, not Tuesday and not Wednesday.

Valerie was thoroughly put out with him by the time she arrived at the attorney's office downtown on Thursday, and she was truly sick of smiling and shrugging with false nonchalance when she reported the lack of communication to her friends every afternoon over coffee. She arrived alone, parked and headed to the office in the square.

The square was a refreshing change from her strip mall in the morning. City Hall sported the only modern facade in the downtown area. Unlike the county seat, however, no turreted and gabled courthouse from a century past commanded the center of the square. That honor was given to a small, white clapboard church and a shady, manicured cemetery that the locals thought of more as a downtown park. No one had been laid to rest there in at least a century, and the church had been converted to a museum in the 1950s. Presided over by an ever-dwindling cadre of matrons and widows, it rarely even opened for viewing, despite the care given its rusty agricultural artifacts. An eclectic mix of shops fronted the square, including a bank, printer, ladies' wear boutique and a variety of gift, antique and other stores. Several of those provided office space above stairs, and it was one of these spaces that the attorney's office occupied.

Valerie entered the street-level door and began the climb up to the suite of offices above a furniture store. She was halfway up when the door opened behind her. Thinking it might be Avis and Sierra, she halted and looked over her shoulder. Ian Keene grinned up at her from the foot of the stairs. Her first thought was that he should always wear that shade of ice-blue. He'd coupled a short-sleeved polo shirt that color with his usual dark jeans, and it made his eyes look positively electric.

Her second thought was that he'd better have a good excuse for not calling, and the third was that Edwin must have mentioned him in the will, after all. It was the second notion that put words in her mouth.

"Well, hello, *stranger.*"

He chuckled, the skunk, and bounded up those stairs like a cowboy-booted cat. "Is that any way to speak to a fellow who has spent the better part of two days and nights figuring out how to replace a dual radiator on a ladder truck?"

"So that leaves just two days to dial a telephone

number. You poor thing. I'm sure you're still working on getting that last digit punched in.''

He stopped on the step beneath her and brought his hands to his hips. "I had work to catch up on, not to mention sleep, but I fully intended to call you yesterday. Then I actually read my mail and realized I'd be seeing you here this morning, so I let it go.''

Before she could follow up on that, the door opened again and Heston Searle loudly proclaimed, ''Oh, good God! What are you two doing here? What has that incompetent old fool done?''

Ian dropped his head forward, muttering, ''Already laying the groundwork, I see.''

Valerie rolled her eyes, arms folding in a stubborn, defensive stance. ''Edwin was *not* incompetent,'' she said forcefully to Heston.

''No?'' Heston shot back, laboriously beginning his climb. ''Then why write a will when we've already got a family trust? It's unbreakable, by the way, so don't even think about trying to cut yourselves in on that.''

''Save your breath, Heston,'' Ian told him, taking Val by the elbow and literally propelling her up to the top of the steps.

As it turned out, Heston needed his breath just to get up those stairs. He came huffing and puffing into the tiny receptionist's office a full half minute after Ian and Valerie had been shown into the attorney's office, where Avis and Sierra already waited. Heston glared at everyone present, slicked down his dark, thinning, oily hair with his palm, and plopped himself down into the nearest chair, which was one of four lining the wall in front of the desk, making it necessary for Ian to seat himself in a chair placed beside the door, perpendicular to the others. The attorney entered the room in a flurry of papers a second later.

Corbett Johnson was a man of indeterminate age. It seemed to Valerie that he'd been practicing here in this cramped office forever and that his had been the image of a perpetually middle-aged man, complete with a slightly receding hairline, touches of distinguished gray at the temples of his medium brown hair, crow's feet at the outside corners of his rather droopy eyes and a bit of jiggle in the jowls. The wobble in his spotted hands, however, left the impression of an older man, and when he put on those enormous owl-eyed glasses of his, he lost a good deal of that stately presence. At the moment, those glasses rode tucked in the buttonhole of his lapel by an earpiece.

He greeted everyone in the room with a handshake, beginning with Avis in the far inside corner. They'd all had dealings with him at one time or another. He'd handled Sierra's divorce and the details that had followed the deaths of Avis's husband and Valerie's father.

"Mrs. Lorimer. Ms. Carlton. Valerie. Heston. Marshal Keene. Very good. We're all here." He walked around the desk, deposited a sheaf of papers there and sat down. "Now, then. Let's get right to it." He shuffled papers into six piles and cleared his throat.

Heston slid to the edge of his seat, declaring loudly, "I want to go on record right now that I'm opposed to this whole thing. My uncle had very little power over the conditions of the trust, just enough to keep me from getting control while he lived, so no matter what you may have told him, he had no need for—''

''Shut up, Heston,'' the attorney said witheringly. ''I've already told you that the trust stands, so rest assured on that score.''

''Then what's the point in all this?'' Heston exclaimed, throwing up his hands. ''The old man didn't have so much as a decent change of clothes so far as I could tell! I didn't even know he had a will.''

Corbett Johnson folded his trembling hands and smiled. That smile was a little chilling. ''He didn't, have a will, that is. Until recently. And Ian, I have to thank you again for bringing him in here.''

All eyes went to Ian Keene, who merely nodded gravely at the attorney.

''You brought my uncle here?'' Heston accused. ''You're behind this? What right have you got interfering in someone else's family matters?''

''Ian didn't interfere in anything,'' Corbett snapped. ''He simply saw a need and took care of it, which is more than anyone can say for you, family or not. Now, I suggest you calm yourself, Mr. Mayor. Edwin has a few surprises in store for you.'' He glanced around the room. ''All of you.''

Heston's eyebrows shot straight up and he settled uneasily in his chair, jaw clamped. Valerie glared silent questions at Ian. What was going on here? Did Ian have anything to do with her and the others being mentioned in the will? Corbett cleared his throat, plucked his glasses from his lapel and shoved them onto his face. Then, picking up a document that he had placed atop the pile squarely in front of him, he began to read aloud.

It was the usual opening, full of legal jargon about sound minds, identity and determined intent. Finally it got down to particulars.

"Item One," the attorney read smoothly, "as pertains to the dispensation of the property, Number 300 County Road 91, sector 7V of the Northwest District plat, Hood County, pertinent to three-quarters of an acre and domicile, one bedroom, one bath, noted outbuildings in itemization and contents, nonitemized, in equal value and control to named heirs, minus and notwithstanding legal claims amounting to four hundred and seventy-nine dollars, Valerie Blunt, Sierra Carlton and Avis Lorimer."

"What does that mean?" Sierra asked, spreading her hands.

Corbett looked at her over the top of his glasses. "He left you three women his house and the lot it sits on."

"His *house?*" Avis erupted in a hushed tone. "He left us his *house?*"

"And all its contents," Corbett said.

Valerie shook her head bemusedly. The old place couldn't be worth much, but Edwin obviously hadn't wanted his nephew to have it, so he'd given it to the three of them just because they'd helped clean up the yard. How wild was that? It was probably going to be more trouble than it was worth, going through all the stuff left in the little house and figuring out what to do with everything, but who knew? They might eventually see a few thousand dollars apiece out of it, provided they could find a buyer, which was a big proviso, considering how many old houses were sitting empty in the area.

"I didn't even know he owned that tumbledown old wreck," Heston sniffed disdainfully. Corbett Johnson glared at him, and Heston turned his head away. Corbett resumed reading.

"Item Two, as pertains to funds deposited with and administered by the Farm and Ranch Bank of Puma Springs, Texas, in the amount of seventeen thousand one hundred eleven dollars cash—"

Heston jerked to the edge of his seat. "What? That old man had seventeen thousand dollars in the bank?"

Ian sat forward and gripped his knees tensely as the attorney cleared his throat and repeated in a loud, determined voice, "Seventeen thousand one hundred eleven dollars *cash, plus* three hundred and eighty thousand dollars in Certificate of Deposit with income amounting to—"

Heston screamed, literally, like a swooning girl at a rock concert. Valerie's mouth dropped open. Corbett, meanwhile, plowed on, but Valerie's stunned ears only caught snatches from then on. Stocks and bonds...six hundred shares...seventeen hundred shares...mineral rights leases...municipal bonds...various funds. Edwin had been wealthy! She thought of all those cheap haircuts she'd given him, of the flowers Sierra had sold him at cost, of the inflated prices Avis had paid him for his old coins, and all the while the old fox had been sitting on a fortune!

"In the total amount of five million seven hundred fifty-four thousand six hundred seventy-three dollars and twenty-two cents, plus accruable interests,'' Corbett concluded. He laid down the will, removed his glasses and mopped his brow with a handkerchief pulled from inside his coat. Everyone else seemed frozen in shock.

For a long moment, no one so much as breathed. Then suddenly Heston sprang to his feet in jubilation. ''Rich!'' he crowed. ''Sweet, merciful God, rich as Midas!''

In a blink, Ian Keene was beside him, one large hand clapped down over Heston's sloped, rounded shoulder. ''Sit,'' he ordered. Heston complied, giggling like a kid turned loose in a candy shop. Ian nodded at Corbett Johnson. ''Go on. Get it over with.''

Corbett put his glasses on once again and bent over the paper on the desk, both hands flattened on the blotter. He cleared his throat nervously and repeated the figure again. ''Five million seven hundred fifty-four thousand six hundred seventy-three dollars and twenty-two cents, plus accruable interests *and* with the exception of fifty thousand dollars cash bequeathed specifically to the Puma Springs Fire Department, to named heirs…'' He took a quick breath and plunged on. ''Valerie Blunt, Sierra Carlton and Avis Lorimer.''

Utter silence followed.

Valerie blinked, not understanding, not daring to understand, what she'd just heard. Then Sierra clamped a hand around Valerie's wrist, squeezing so tightly that Val could feel the throb of her own pulse. At the same time Avis made a squeaky, inarticulate noise that sounded part disbelief and part dismay. It finally sunk in when Corbett removed his glasses, looked up and announced gently, "Congratulations, ladies. After taxes, I'd say you've inherited just over a million dollars each."

Everyone reacted at once. Sierra clapped both hands over her mouth, while Avis gasped, "No!" Valerie swayed in her seat, sudden tears filling her eyes. Dear God in heaven. Millionaires. Edwin had made them, her, millionaires! Heston suddenly squealed like a stuck pig, twisting and writhing in his seat beneath the pressure of Ian's staying hand.

As if from a distance, Val heard Heston screaming that it wasn't right, couldn't be right. He insisted that he was the only heir. His uncle couldn't have that much money, but if he had, it surely belonged to Heston. "I'm family! I ought to be in that will!"

"You are," Corbett calmly assured him. Flipping up a couple of pages, he quickly read, "Item Three, as to the Searle Land Trust, established April 1931, and being the legal property of siblings Edwin Hale Searle and Emma Searle Witt, Emma Searle Witt no longer being of sound mind and her wishes previously made known and legally attested, devolves to her surviving heir, Heston Searle Witt, with the additional amount, deposited in trust from the estate of the said Edwin Hale Searle, of one dollar."

"One dollar!" Heston screamed, sliding toward the floor only at the last moment to pop up onto his feet. "One dollar? Out of millions? I don't think so! No. Uh-uh!"

"You got the land, Heston," Corbett pointed out.

"That's what you've always wanted, what you've always expected, and all you're legally entitled to. The rest was Edwin's to dispose of as he saw fit, and I quite approve of his dispensation."

"It's not true!" Heston whirled, knocking over a pencil jar on Corbett's desk, and jabbed a finger at the three women still sitting in shock. "You're not going to get away with this!" He was blubbering now, crying like a baby. "I'll take you to court! I'll...I'll find out how you managed this, and I'll expose you all!"

"That's enough," Ian said quietly.

Heston jerked around. "You! I'll have your job for this! I'm not the mayor for nothing!"

"Oh, yes, you are," Corbett said. "I know it's a blow, Heston, discovering your poor old uncle wasn't poor, after all, but there is nothing you can do about any of this. Take the land and be happy with it, because that's all you're going to get."

"We'll see about that," Heston snarled. "I have friends, influence. He was crazy. You all knew! Somehow you found out about the money, and you took advantage of a crazy old man!"

"Okay, we need a little break here," Ian said, seizing Heston by the elbow and hauling him toward the door. "You can come back and sign the papers after you calm down."

"I'll sign nothing!" Heston declared, digging in his heels.

"Then you won't get the ranch deed in your control," Corbett pointed out.

"I'll have you disbarred!" Heston threatened

shrilly, stabbing a finger at the attorney. Corbett just shook his head as Ian clapped hands down on Heston's shoulders and propelled him bodily to the door.

"You'll pay for this!" Heston yelled as Ian pushed him out into the receiving room. "You'll all pay for this!" They could hear him sobbing as Ian escorted him through the outer room and ejected him onto the staircase.

"Well," Corbett Johnson said, leaning back in his chair. "I actually expected him to faint when he heard the news."

"I may do that myself," Avis gasped.

"I can't believe this!" Sierra exclaimed.

Valerie felt tears rolling down her face. The same question had begun circling in her mind. *Why? Why?*

"Edwin did this for us. Oh, my God." She felt Sierra's hand clasp hers and knew that she was doing the same with Avis. Emotion overwhelmed her, a jumbled, roiling wave of relief, amazement, grief, gratitude, doubt, even guilt. "We don't deserve this," she said. "We...I was just *nice* to him, that's all, and sometimes it wasn't very easy. Sometimes I had to dig deep for the patience to be nice to him."

Corbett smiled. "I understand. So did he. Edwin wasn't always easy to be nice to, but the three of you always managed, and he valued that." The attorney sat forward, folding his arms against the top edge of his desk. "Look, Edwin had no family other than Heston, and he frankly didn't want our illustrious mayor to get anything that the law doesn't mandate. All his closest friends are at the ends of their lives. They don't need money at this point. And why should he leave his wealth to some anonymous charity when the three of you, all single women with certain weighty responsibilities and limited means, had won special places in his heart with your uncommon kindnesses? It makes a lovely kind of sense, if you ask me.'' He began pulling papers from the stacks before him and turned them toward the women, saying, ''Now I want you all to sign these papers, then go out and celebrate. Edwin would've liked that.''

He laid out pens, but for some time, no one reached for them. Then, slowly, one by one, Sierra first, then Avis and finally Val, the women picked up the pens and started signing. Valerie's hand shook so that she could barely read her own signature, but she scribbled her name everywhere that Corbett indicated. When they were done, the fastidious attorney carefully replaced every page back in the proper order in each stack. Then he pushed up from his desk and sighed with satisfaction.

''I'll have the will filed with the probate court by the end of the business day. It'll take some time for everything to play out, but they're expecting you down at the bank whenever you're ready. You can expect sizable loans with excellent terms to help bridge the time gap should you need them. But that's up to you. I hope you'll each follow my advice and get some expert financial counsel before you make any important purchases or decisions. Congratulations again, ladies. I'm happy to have been able to do this for Edwin and the three of you.''

Valerie got up and turned blindly for the door, her head swimming. She walked straight into Ian Keene.

"Congratulations, hon," he said, hugging her. He turned her face up with a crooked finger and dropped a light kiss on her mouth. "I'm so pleased for you."

Valerie nodded, a strange numbness spreading through her as elation warred with shock and disbelief. She wondered vaguely if it was a dream and made her way foggily into the outer room. Stumbling, she found herself on the stairs, heading down toward the street. Someone said, "Watch your step."

The next thing she knew, she was sitting behind the wheel of her car, staring through the windshield, and Ian Keene was crouched down beside her in the open door, asking, "You okay?"

"I don't know," she answered honestly. "I don't know."

"Give yourself some time," he said. "Haven't I been telling you that everything would be okay?"

"Have you?" Valerie remarked absently, turning her gaze on him.

He just smiled and patted her knee. A chill swept through her. He had been telling her. He had known. She couldn't think why, just then, that this was important. All she knew was that everything had changed.

Chapter Seven

"I can't believe it," Gwyn said for perhaps the fifth time.

"Millions," Avis whispered with a shake of her head.

"What I don't understand is why," Valerie said, once more giving voice to the question that had plagued her since she'd found out about this incredible inheritance the three of them shared. "Why leave all that money to us?"

"You heard what the attorney said," Sierra insisted. "We're all single women struggling financially. Who better to leave it to?"

"Because we were kind to him," Avis said, a note of wonder in her voice.

"But that's just it," Valerie argued. "We didn't

even have to be kind to him. He could afford to pay fair prices!"

"It wasn't about money," Avis objected gently. "It was never about money, not for me. Yes, I thought he was poor, but more than anything else I realized that he had no one to care about him."

"Devotion," Sierra murmured, a faraway look in her eye. "It was his devotion that got to me. Rich or poor, every week he took flowers to his sister and wife. Neither of them knew, could know. But that didn't keep him from performing that simple act of devotion steadily. I had to honor that, even if he was a little grumpy. Dear heaven, does that kind of devotion even exist anymore?"

Valerie nodded her understanding. "I always thought he was lonely, and that he pretended to be gruff to cover it. I couldn't ignore that."

"Oh, for pity's sake!" Gwyn snapped. "That old man took advantage of you all. He knew you needed money, but he let you two sell services and products below cost and cheated Avis out of the extra money she gave him for those moldy old coins! He was hateful to everyone who crossed his path, and he left you that money out of pure spite!"

"That's not fair. How's bequeathing millions spiteful?" Sierra retorted.

"Because he just didn't want his nephew to get it!" Gwyn shouted back.

"Then why not leave it all to some charity or the town or even the government?" Avis reasoned impassionedly. "Why leave it to us three?"

"Because he had a guilty conscience, that's why,"

Gwyn insisted. "You three were the only ones stupid enough to let him take advantage of you, the hateful old son of a—"

"Stop it!" Valerie yelled, appalled at what she saw happening.

Gwyn paled and covered her mouth with one hand. "Oh, God. I can't believe how jealous I sound!"

Sierra, Avis and Valerie looked at one another, a new concern in all their eyes. The coffee shop door opened and half a dozen people streamed in. One of them was Janine Hensley, a client of Valerie's. She made a beeline to the table.

"I just heard! The mayor himself stopped me on the street with the news! Can you believe it? What're you going to do with all that money?"

"Your lucky day, huh?" someone else said. "Wish I'd known that old man was worth a mint!"

"What'd you have to do to get it?" another voice asked, failing to allow time for an answer. "Whatever it was, I'd have done it, too, for a million bucks!"

Discussion started at the counter about a popular movie where a man was offered a million dollars for a single night with his wife. Gwyn dashed tears from her eyes with the hem of her apron and busily began taking orders in a stern voice that let everyone know that mere loiterers were not welcome.

Valerie looked at Sierra and Avis worriedly. An odd lethargy had settled upon her, an exhaustion born, no doubt, of emotional overload, and she just couldn't seem to sort out her feelings, but she very much feared what Edwin had unleashed. Then Buddy walked in the door, a familiar spring in his step, and she groaned aloud.

He threw out his arms and shouted, "Hey, babe! Oooee!" Bounding over to the table, he scooped her up in a bear hug. She fought her way free while he chortled about "their" good fortune and how clever she'd been in playing up to "that old grouch." He showed not an instant's hesitation or offense when she ordered him to get away from her. Instead he threw his head back and crowed, "This is so cool!"

Sierra and Avis got to their feet, the looks on their faces saying that they were as appalled by this attention as she was. Sierra began pushing past Buddy at the end of the table to the aisle, Avis right behind her. When Derrick Albert, the one-man staff of the local newspaper, entered the now crowded coffee shop, notepad in hand, Sierra stopped in her tracks and did an abrupt about-face.

Buddy, bless his helpful little heart, waved a hand and called, "Here! Here they are, the new millionaires of Puma Springs!"

Valerie began to wish that the floor would open up and swallow her as Derrick made his way toward them. A big man somewhere in his forties, he moved with the lumbering agility of a bear newly awakened from hibernation, an image fostered by the perpetual disarray of his medium brown hair and ubiquitous khaki clothing, including a safari vest with numerous pockets, tabs and rings. Derrick considered himself a veteran newsman, though in truth he'd inherited the paper from his elderly aunt only a few years earlier. Until then he'd managed the local hardware store.

"Just the girls I wanted to see," he announced glibly. "So how's it feel to be instant millionaires?"

Sierra put a hand to her head. Val closed her eyes. Only Avis, forever polite, answered. "It, uh, hasn't really sunk in yet."

"Did you know the old boy had money?"

All three of them answered firmly, "No!"

"Okay, okay, just asking. Because, you know, there are those who are saying you did." They looked at one another. Heston had been very busy. "So what're you going to do with the money?" Derrick asked. "Giving anything to charity?"

"How about the town," somebody else asked. "You gonna give anything to the town?"

"We could use a new city hall."

"No, a park. We ain't got a park in this whole town besides that graveyard."

"Aw, the government's gonna get most of it anyway. Why should they give it to the town? Me, I'd buy some things."

"Yeah, like a million lottery tickets." Laughter followed this.

"A car," Buddy said, getting his wish on the list, "something low and sleek and fast as a jet."

Valerie glanced at her co-inheritors and saw her own dismay and sadness reflected there. "Has it occurred to anyone," Avis said with soft-spoken conviction, "that an old man has died?"

"A rich old man," Buddy qualified, grinning like a cat in cream.

Valerie put all her disdain into the look she turned on him then. "An old man who was so lonely in this town that he gave his money to three women who had simply treated him with common courtesy and a little patience.''

"If you ask me," Sierra added, "that's not something to be happy about."

"So you don't want the money?" Derrick pressed.

Before Sierra could answer, someone cracked, "Hoo, boy, the mayor would sure be tickled to hear that." General laughter followed. Sierra looked at Val and Avis and started for the door, pushing past Buddy and Derrick Albert. Avis fell in behind her, and Valerie brought up the rear, shaken by the speed with which the news had spread and the general avidity of those who had heard it. Buddy followed hot on her heels.

"Hey, I have some more questions," Derrick called out to them, and the growing crowd in the coffee shop started shouting suggestions at him.

Valerie heard Janine Hensley demand eagerly, "Ask if anybody's going to have cosmetic surgery."

"Oh, my God," Sierra said, hitting the sidewalk. She turned around, walking backward to put distance between herself and the crowd in the coffee shop and still address her friends. "I can't believe this is happening."

"Believe it," Valerie muttered, catching up to her.

They stopped a little way down the sidewalk and waited for Avis to join them. "I'm beginning to think that Edwin might not have done us as much of a favor as he intended," she said quietly.

"What are we going to do?" Sierra wanted to know.

"Do?" Buddy echoed, once more interjecting himself into the group. "Why, sugar, the whole point of being rich is that you don't have to do anything at all if you don't want to."

"It would be as far as you're concerned," Valerie retorted, "but then the rest of us aren't lazy jerks."

"Oh, baby, don't be like that," he cajoled, draping an arm around her shoulder. "You know you don't mean it, and besides, you need your old friends around you now. You won't be able to trust the new ones."

A familiar chill ran through her. "It's true that we've known each other a long time, Buddy, so long that I can read you like a book. Don't think for a minute that anything's changed between us."

"'Course not. You know I've always been crazy about you."

Valerie laughed at him. The jerk. "You are so transparent. You think that because I'm going to have money you don't have to pay me for the dent you put in my car, so everything just ought to be forgotten and forgiven. Well, I may have been born at night, but it wasn't last night. This is all about the money and not your fake feelings."

"Hey, this is good old Buddy here, not Johnny-on-the-spot Ian Keene."

That pesky chill suddenly intensified to the status of an Arctic blast. "What the devil does that mean?"

Buddy bounced his weight on one foot, head bobbing rhythmically. "Stands to reason, doesn't it? I mean, everybody knows he found all that cash of Edwin's."

"What cash?" Sierra asked.

"When he inspected the place. I heard he found bonds and boxes and bags of money in the house, thousands, they're saying. He insisted old Edwin take it down to the bank. He probably knew there was more and that's why he got the old man to make out a will." Valerie heard a strange whistling in her ears, like a missile coming in to strike a target. "He probably thought he could get himself in the will," Buddy sneered, "and when he couldn't, he went after you. Don't you see, Val? He knew before he ever tried to get between us, before he ever asked you out. He knew you were in the will. He had to."

The truth of it hit Valerie in a blow as devastating as any bomb. He knew. He had always known. Why else had he even been present at the reading of the will this morning?

"Haven't I been telling you that everything would work out okay?"

She closed her eyes. Suddenly everything that had happened between them seemed sinister and telling. He hadn't liked her any better than she'd liked him in the beginning. Then he'd found out about Edwin's will, and he had changed. She looked at her friends, saw the outrage and pity in their eyes and knew herself for the greatest of fools. But of course she was. She'd gone around year after year with the likes of Buddy Wilcox, for pity's sake. She must have seemed like easy pickings to Ian, which was probably why he'd come after her instead of Avis and Sierra, both of whom were older and more experienced.

Her stomach began to churn, and she realized that

she was in very real danger of throwing up. Without a word, she turned and headed for her car, dismissing the salon and everything in it as unimportant in the larger scheme of her life.

"Valerie," Avis called, her voice thick with concern.

"Hey, Val, wait!" Buddy exclaimed, running after her.

She stopped long enough to round on him, hissing, "Stay away from me. I mean it. Far, far away."

She left him standing there with his hands on his hips and his mouth hanging open. No doubt existed in her mind that it was the right thing to do, even if she suddenly felt more alone than she ever had in her life.

"I thought you must be busy," Ian said, closing the salon door gently behind him and nodding at the chairs filled with waiting clients. "You haven't been answering your phone."

Valerie lowered her arms, comb in one hand, curling iron in the other, and looked away from the teenager whose long hair she was styling. "Funny," she said, "my appointment book is suddenly full. Go figure."

"Nothing works like money," Ian commented, smiling once more over her good fortune. "You must still be getting used to the idea."

"Some things you don't ever get used to," she muttered, working doggedly.

Momentarily taken aback by her sullenness, Ian looked down at the toes of his boots. Well, he'd known it would be a shock. Time would take care of it, but in the meanwhile perhaps a quiet dinner in some out-of-the-way spot would help to relieve the stress. He had a couple of places in mind, but he didn't much like the idea of asking her out in front of all these avid observers. He tried his hand at small talk.

"You know, all the time I was working on that ladder truck, I kept thinking that if the darn thing had broken down just a few weeks later, I could've spared myself the headache and paid someone else to do it, but I guess it's better this way. Even in our little department, old Edwin's fifty-thousand-dollar bequest won't go as far as we'd like."

She turned on him with that hot iron in her hand. "Is that all you can think about? A man has died, but just because he left a little money everyone seems to have forgotten that fact."

"A *little* money?" he heard himself echo and winced inwardly, knowing that it was precisely the wrong thing to say. She was still grieving Edwin and, no doubt, feeling guilty about her unexpected inheritance.

"All right, a lot of money," she snapped. "That just makes what you did worse."

"What I did?" He shook his head, at a complete loss. "I don't get it."

"Obviously. And you won't, either."

"Huh?"

"I'm not the fool you think I am, Ian, and you're not as smart as you think you are."

Now that was downright personal. And unjustified. Whatever it meant. "What's got into you?"

"As if you didn't know."

He opened his mouth to retort that he couldn't possibly know what idiotic notion she had rattling around inside that head of hers now, but a movement that he caught out of the corner of his eye reminded him that they were not alone. He swallowed the angry rejoinder, turned on his heel and walked right out the same way he'd come in.

Sheesh! What kind of burr did she have under her saddle today? He'd thought these misunderstandings and erroneous conclusions were behind them, a product of her intense financial difficulties, but apparently not. What was her excuse this time? he wondered. Maybe she just figured he was beneath her now that she had real money, but somehow he didn't think that was it.

He'd pretty much convinced himself that she was just the girl for him. They'd had a great time together on their night out, and he'd relived that steamy hot kiss a dozen times since. Maybe she was a little young, but he'd been willing to make allowances for that since she didn't seem to have any particular interest in marriage. Otherwise, why would she have wasted all those years on the likes of Buddy Wilcox? Maybe that was the problem. Maybe she cared for Buddy more than she wanted anyone to know, but if that was the case, how did he explain that explosive kiss the other night?

He shook his head and slammed his way into his truck. The woman was simply unfathomable. Nothing about her added up as it should. She wasn't even his type physically—except somehow she was. Operative word: was. Apparently it was over. He should consider himself lucky that it hadn't gone far. A spunky, independent woman was one thing; a rich, spunky, independent woman was another, and he was well rid, obviously, of that complication. So be it. A woman never figured into his life for long, anyway, so what difference did it make? None whatsoever.

Except somehow it did.

Valerie climbed the steps of her mother's front porch—this house would always be home. She'd grown up here, and it was here that she'd sat beside her mother and brother and listened to the highway patrolman explain how her father had rolled his car down an embankment while trying to pass a slower vehicle on the shoulder of the road.

Her current misery was a distant second, because everything had changed that day. One moment her world had been a familiar one of pom-poms and homework and Friday night football games, and the next it had become a nightmare of unrealistic proportions and bizarre problems like how to manage a prom dress for herself and new shoes for Dillon at the same time. Valerie never came home that she didn't think of that day or how they had struggled to hold on to this place after discovering that her father had cashed in his life insurance to finance another of his investment schemes.

Now, suddenly, her life had been forever altered again, financial status included, and she was afraid to be happy about it. She didn't dare trust it. How could she forget that in order for her to have money a man had died? Worse, how did she know who to trust now? Like Ian. He had known. All along, he had known, and she couldn't forget that.

She let herself in the front door and walked through her mother's shabby living room, intensely aware of every threadbare spot in the decades-old furniture. As she skirted her grandmother's dining room suite and the built-in china cabinets containing a life's worth of cheap knickknacks, she could hear her mother humming in the kitchen.

Usually when she first entered this room the years fell away like magic and a sense of well-being temporarily enveloped her. Today the dull, pale blue cabinets, plain white walls and worn linoleum seemed depressing and out of kilter. Delores Blunt turned to her daughter with a wide smile, her gray-streaked, dark blond hair waving about her plump, pretty face.

"Oh, I'm so glad to see you." She left a mess of green beans, which she was washing, in the sink and came forward, wiping her hands on her apron, to give Valerie a hug.

"Mama."

"How are you, honey?"

"I don't know."

"Still can't believe it? I can't, either. It's almost like when your daddy died."

"Yes."

"Your brother's on his way home, by the way."

Valerie sighed. "You know he's failed two more classes."

"Well, we won't worry about that now. We have other food on our plate just at the moment, and quite a feast it is, too. You seem tired."

"I didn't sleep much again last night," Valerie admitted. "I just keep thinking about Edwin."

"Valerie, I want you to listen to me," Delores said, taking both of her daughter's hands in hers. "I've always been proud of you. Always. I don't know what I'd have done without you when your father died. Sometimes I think I depended on you too much, Dillon and I both, but you've never complained. You have a good heart, Val, and I know that's why you dealt with old Mr. Searle the way you did, and that's why he left you the money. You think you don't deserve it, but I'd like to know who deserves it more?"

"I know, Mom. It's just… I got the money because he died."

"And you're still grieving him," Delores said, folding her close again, "just as you're still grieving your father after all these years."

Valerie bit her lip. "Are you telling me I shouldn't grieve?"

"I'm telling you that I don't believe Edwin left you that money in order to make you miserable. He did it to make you happy, Val, and also to throw a little excitement into your life. Think of all the good that money's going to do, and be happy about that, at least."

"You're right," Val said. "I have a lot to be happy about," but she added silently, *"even if I can't trust Ian."*

They both became aware of a deep, throbbing rumble. As it drew quickly closer, the glass in the window above the sink rattled. Valerie turned in that direction the same moment as her mother and caught sight of something hurtling past along the drive.

"What on earth?" Delores exclaimed, starting for the back door.

The rumble died just as they got the door opened and stuck their heads out. A motorcycle stood beside the stoop, its black-clad rider just dismounting. Valerie knew even before he reached up and pushed off his helmet that she was looking at her brother Dillon's latest folly.

"Good grief, what now?" Delores said, parking her fists at her ample hips.

Dillon shook out his curly, sandy-brown hair, a sardonic look on his thin face. "Good to see you, too, Mom, Sis. Whatever happened to 'Welcome home'?"

"Where'd you get the bike, Dillon?" Valerie demanded.

"And what happened to your car?" Delores added.

He shrugged. "I traded."

Valerie stepped out onto the stoop and looked down at the big, shiny bike. "You're telling me that you traded that old heap of yours for this brand new bike, even?"

"No, of course not," Dillon admitted easily, that contemptuous grin of his slipping into place.

"So how did you make up the difference?" Delores wanted to know.

"Took out a loan, of course."

"You couldn't buy a pack of chewing gum on credit," Valerie pointed out.

That grin widened. "I can now."

Valerie folded her arms. "Who told you about the money?"

He laughed. "Are you kidding? Everybody I know has called to tell me about it! Way to go, Sis."

Anger erupted inside Valerie. Way to go? As if she'd maneuvered Edwin into leaving her a million bucks! As if she'd worked for this, expected this, manipulated this. She pointed a trembling finger at the bike. "I'm not paying for that motorcycle."

"It didn't cost *that* much," Dillon argued. "Twenty-five thousand with my car. That's a drop in the bucket to you now."

"I'm not paying for it, Dillon. I mean it. You might as well take it back right now because you're not getting a nickel out of me for that thing."

"Oh, isn't that just like you!" Dillon yelled. "Me, me, me."

"Dillon, that's unfair," Delores scolded.

"No, it isn't. She's always held the purse strings, always decided who got what!"

"Maybe because I've always brought in the cash that filled the purse!" Valerie shouted.

"And do you ever let me forget it?" Dillon retorted. "Ever since Dad died, you've made sure we all knew what you had to give up, what you had to do to provide."

"That's not true!" Delores exclaimed.

Dillon ignored her, shouting at Valerie, "It's not enough that you got all his attention when he was alive, you had to take his place once he was dead and keep reminding me that I'm nothing!"

Valerie reeled backward, the air *whooshing* out of her as if she'd taken a roundhouse to the solar plexus.

"Dillon!" Delores gasped.

Before Valerie could get her breath, Dillon jammed the helmet on his head, jumped on the bike and took off again.

"He didn't mean that," Delores said to Valerie. But he did. They both knew he did. "Somehow he got it in his head that you were Daddy's favorite," Delores explained plaintively, twisting her hands together. "I've told him time and time again, but I just don't think he can hear it."

Valerie closed her eyes. Daddy's little girl. Daddy's princess. She had been their father's favorite, his adoring, adored favorite. Even Ian could tell. Ian.

She gasped in pain, and the anger came rushing back again, but this time she was angry with her father. It wasn't enough that he had adored her. He'd taken stupid risks all the time, believing himself invulnerable because he had the courage, the poor judgment, to pass vehicles on the wrong side, jump off a roof into a swimming pool on a dare, learn to blow fire out of his mouth with the aid of a cigarette lighter and bet everything they owned on one wild scheme after another. He'd disdained his son because Dillon had been a quiet, sensitive child more like their mother, and for that, too, Valerie wanted to shake him, but she couldn't.

Over the years, Dillon had done everything in his power to live up to their father's wild reputation. How far, she wondered, would he go?

"I'll find him," she told her mother woodenly, "bring him home safe."

Delores Blunt nodded, just as if she believed Valerie could actually do that. Hurrying from the house, one hand clutching her stomach, Valerie fought the urge to sob. Crying would solve nothing and neither, she understood bleakly, would money, no matter how much she wanted to believe that it could.

Chapter Eight

Valerie glanced at her wristwatch. Half past eleven. She'd looked everywhere she could think to look for her brother, gone by all his friends' places, checked out his favorite hangouts. In the end, she'd driven around aimlessly hoping for some chance glimpse of him. Finally, she'd come back here, convinced her mother to go to bed and taken up her post as sentinel on the front porch steps. The incredible beauty of the night was wasted on her, however. All she could think about was Dillon. She imagined him lying mangled on some lonely roadside. Folding her forearms across the tops of her knees, she bowed her head against them.

A few moments later, something cold touched the palm of her hand. Jerking upright, she was greeted by a friendly *whuff* and the doggy smile of the owner of a cold, black nose. She frowned in recognition. "What are you doing here?"

The long, heavy tail thumped on the walkway, and Valerie scratched a pointed, black ear even as she looked beyond the dog. Ian stood at the end of the walk, a wary expression on his face.

"Was that question for me?"

She suppressed an instant of excitement, of hope, and dropped her gaze to the dog, rubbing its big, flat skull. "I don't think this guy's going to answer me."

Ian walked forward. "We're just going back home. Cato likes a late walk before turning in for the night."

"Home?"

He stopped and pointed to his right. "Yeah, I leased a house three doors down."

She mentally counted off the houses in that direction. "The Philpot place?"

He shook his head. "Landlord's name is Holden."

"That's the Philpots' daughter and son-in-law. They inherited the place after…" Valerie looked away, reminded of her own inheritance.

Ian strolled closer. "So you know the neighborhood?"

"I grew up here. My mom still lives in this house."

He smoothed his hands down the slopes of his thighs. "I haven't really gotten to know the neighbors. Haven't had time."

"Busy witnessing wills, I guess," she jibed flippantly.

He turned a frown on her. "I know you're upset with me. I just don't know why. Because I witnessed Edwin's will?"

She looked away, trying to convey both disdain and lack of concern. "I just can't help wondering how you came to that. I mean, you hardly hit town before you're privy to an old man's secrets and witnessing his will. Lots of people are curious about that, you know."

Ian's hands fisted, then relaxed again. "Lots of people can go hang," he said, "but if you really want to know, I was just doing my job."

She arched an eyebrow at him. "Just doing your job. Sounds familiar."

"Look, as soon as I got hired I drew up an inspection schedule for commercial properties and drove around town making a list of the residential problem spots. Edwin's place was at the top of the residential list, so I started there."

"Naturally," she echoed snidely, quite aware of how ardent he could be in the pursuit of his job. He chose to ignore that and went on.

"Edwin fought me on it, of course, but I'd had the foresight to go armed with a legal writ. Once I got a good look around, I knew why he didn't want me or anyone else in there. I could not believe what I found hidden around the place. It was stuffed in boxes and bags, under the furniture, in the closet and cabinets. It was even in his dresser drawers."

"Cash."

He didn't seem surprised that she knew. "It was mostly single dollar bills, quite a few fives, nothing larger than a ten, and more coins than I could possibly have counted."

"So you made him take it to the bank."

"I didn't *make* him do anything," Ian protested. "But surely you see how dangerous it was for him to keep all that cash in the house with him, not to mention the fire hazard of all that paper money."

"Okay," she conceded, "so you *convinced* him to take it to the bank."

"It wasn't easy. He was ticked at me for making the inspection in the first place. But eventually I got through to him. When we got to the bank, though, the director took me and Edwin into his office, informed me of the extent of Edwin's estate and begged me, in front of Edwin, to convince the old man to make out a will. He seemed to think I had some special influence over the old guy."

"Obviously he was right."

Ian lifted a hand to the back of his neck, saying, "Not really. All I did was apply a little reverse psychology."

Valerie narrowed her eyes. "In what way?"

Ian shrugged. "The problem, apparently, was that Edwin couldn't decide what to do with his money. He didn't want Heston to have it, but he was concerned that his sister wouldn't receive the care she needs if he left the money out of the family. The banker tried to tell him that it didn't have to be that way, but the more he argued, the more Edwin dug in his heels, so finally I just said that I didn't see a problem, that our nice mayor ought to get it all and that surely he would look after his own mother, so why bother with a will?"

Valerie rolled her eyes. "I can just imagine how that went over."

Ian pinched the bridge of his nose with his thumb and forefinger. "If I'd known about Edwin's health problems, I wouldn't have said it. He got so mad that he nearly had a heart attack right then. I could tell because of my EMT training, not that I'm fully qualified, but I know the danger signs. Once I got him calmed down, he confessed what his doctor had told him a few weeks earlier. Apparently he'd been dealing with a heart condition for some time, and it had progressed to the point of no return. Didn't seem to be anything else they could do for him. The banker and I convinced him that he just couldn't wait any longer—unless he really did want Heston to get everything."

So far, his explanation seemed completely plausible, but he hadn't told her what she really needed to know yet. "So you took him to the attorney."

"He asked me to go with him, and later he asked me to witness the will. I was glad to do it."

"And he paid you back with a $50,000 bequest to the fire department."

"I didn't know about that until the will was read. That part was added later. Corbett will tell you the same thing if you ask."

She looked down at her hands in the yellow glow of the porch light as they patted the dog, which had settled himself between her feet. "How did he come to settle on Sierra, Avis and me as beneficiaries?"

Ian shrugged. "The lawyer kept talking about charities and municipal trusts and what have you, but that just seemed to irritate Edwin, so I told him to give it to whomever he felt most deserved and needed it."

Ian smiled then and told her, "Edwin said you three together—you three *'gals'*—were worth the whole rest of the town. Corbett seemed to agree, and that was it."

She looked at him. "Just like that?"

"Just like that."

"You didn't try to change his mind?"

"Why would I? It was none of my business. I'll confess that later I was pleased to see that the three of you really did care for him, but it wouldn't have mattered to me if he'd left the whole kit and caboodle to Heston. It was no skin off my nose either way."

"Because you had an in with the mayor?"

He drew back at that, his face screwing into a frown. "What?"

"I know the mayor was a supporter of yours," she went on pointedly. "I talked to him myself."

"So? He's no supporter of mine now. He's already tried to have me fired."

"Because of the will."

Ian shrugged. "We'd have come to loggerheads about something sometime. Heston's like that."

She couldn't argue with Ian's assessment of their mayor. No one got along with Heston all the time because no one else had Heston's best interests at heart all the time, except perhaps his equally shallow and selfish wife. No, Heston would never have proven a reliable conduit to Edwin's money for Ian. She, on the other hand, might have. That knowledge pierced her to the core, and she heard herself blurting, "Why did you ask me out?"

Ian blinked at her. "For the usual reasons."

"Apparently the usual reasons only applied after you knew about the will."

He tilted his head slowly as if not certain he'd heard her correctly. Then suddenly he threw up his arms. "If that doesn't take the flipping cake!"

"You didn't even ask until after he died!" she argued, leaping to her feet.

He pivoted on one heel. "I didn't ask until I had at least some reason to think you'd agree to go out with me! Or have you forgotten that I was at the top of your enemies list when we first met?"

True. But it didn't negate the possibility he'd played up to her and had been thinking about the money as he'd done so.

"I haven't forgotten anything," she muttered, folding her arms. It was all too true. She remembered with uncommon vividness every moment she'd spent with this man.

"Cato!" he snapped, striding down her mother's walk. "Come!" The dog turned his head in Ian's direction and whined plaintively. Suddenly, Ian wheeled again and pointed a finger at her. "You know what's sad about this? We could've really had something. That's what's sad." He stomped his foot. "Cato!" The dog got up, ears laid back, and stared at his master as if trying to decide whether or not to obey his command.

"Go on," Valerie muttered to the dog, nudging it with her foot. "Go on home where you belong."

"Cato, heel!" Ian ordered sharply, and this time the big dog reluctantly trotted down the path.

Valerie watched the pair fade into the shadows beneath the trees that lined the street and thought about what he'd said. After a few moments, she hunkered down again on the top step to wait for her brother, but her worry for him had now been embroidered with disappointment, doubt and a loneliness so heavy that even the deepening, much longed for rumble of the motorcycle engine as it neared did not lift her gloom. She had always believed that the lack of money was the only reason for her lack of happiness, but she knew now that it wasn't so. As she went to greet her brother, she felt as powerless as ever to change what hurt her most.

"That's a Japanese camera crew filming in front of Avis's hobby shop," Gwyn said, clearly amazed. "I swear, the world has turned upside down."

Ian was inclined to agree—his world had certainly flip-flopped—but he said nothing, merely sipped his coffee and brooded over the past few days.

"Instant Millionaires!" The headline had run on the front page of the local paper the day after the reading of the will. The next day a television film crew from Fort Worth had showed up, and Valerie, Sierra and Avis had sat down with them to talk about Edwin and the inheritance. The heavily edited version that had run on the evening news had made them sound like brainless twits and featured a shot of Heston proclaiming his uncle's questionable state of mind.

The day after that, the town had been swamped by reporters from every Dallas and Fort Worth media venue. It didn't take a genius to realize that the more they said, the more ammunition they gave to those who would twist their words in order to build interest in the story, so Val, Sierra and Avis had wisely made themselves scarce.

On their behalf, Corbett Johnson had issued a joint statement in which the three women had expressed their shock and gratitude at Edwin's largesse and tried to convey what he had meant to them. They had made it clear that they'd had no notion of Edwin's worth and had, in fact, considered him the next thing to a pauper. In the end, however, all they'd done was give Heston another chance to insist otherwise.

Valerie's idiotic little brother had gotten himself and his flashy new motorcycle on the news, declaring that he was sure his sister was going to buy their mother a new house. Delores Blunt had countered that there was nothing wrong with the house she had, prompting a reporter to suggest that her daughter was too cheap to set up her mom in new digs. Reporters had shoved microphones in the face of Sierra's little daughter, Tyree, on her way home from school and made much of Avis's May-December marriage to her late husband. Gwyn had barred the media from her coffee shop as a result.

Now they had taken to filming exterior shots at any spot with connections to the three heiresses, their homes, businesses, favorite restaurants, churches, even Edwin's graveside. Some idiot had actually gone to the high school and interviewed some of the old teachers about Valerie's years there. This had inevitably led them to Buddy Wilcox, who couldn't say enough about his own high school football career or his long relationship with Valerie, whom he painted as a party girl. It all made Ian sick.

Shoving aside his uneaten sweet roll and empty coffee cup, he got up from the bar stool, tossed a few bills on the counter and went out. Gwyn barely glanced at the plate before whisking it and the cup away. Ian sensed that she was as troubled by the inheritance and the resulting chaos as the heiresses themselves. Sighing inwardly, he trudged over to his truck, got inside and drove away.

Ian saw the camera truck parked haphazardly in front of the fire station long before he got there. For a moment, he considered just driving on by, but it was inevitable that they should get to him eventually, and he knew that under the right circumstances he could set straight several facts that the mayor had skewed. Besides, it was obvious that Brent had his hands full with this bunch. When Ian got out of the truck and pocketed his keys, Brent sent him an anxious glance. Ian nodded, and Brent pointed in his direction with obvious relief. A cadaverously thin blonde with unnaturally plump lips and heavy makeup hurried toward him, followed by two men, one with a camera on his shoulder and the other carrying a clipboard and wearing headphones with an attached mouthpiece.

Ian pointed to the cameraman and said flatly, "You keep that lens capped until I come to an agreement with Ms. Chasen or you're out of here."

The woman preened. "So you know me."

"I watch the national newsmagazine shows from time to time."

"We just want to ask you about the part you played in the writing of Edwin Searle's will."

"And I'll tell you," Ian said, "provided I get to see and approve the final cut before the piece airs."

She gave him a patently false smile. "We can't do that."

He turned toward the firehouse, tossing over his shoulder, "See ya."

"Wait. Wait, Marshal Keene. Maybe we can work something out."

Ian stopped and turned to face her. "Work it out in writing," he instructed. "There have been enough distortion, innuendo and false accusations made already. When you have the necessary guarantee on paper, you know where to find me." With that he turned back toward the firehouse.

The news team was on its way to their van when a car screeched around the corner and came to a halt in the street. The mayor jumped out and ran toward them, puffing in his ill-fitted suit. He pointed at Ian but addressed Ms. Chasen. "Whatever he's told you, I demand an opportunity to refute it."

"I haven't told them anything," Ian snapped, "and neither will you."

"You're not going to shut me up, Keene. I've been robbed, and this whole town knows it!"

Ian brought his hands to his hips and looked down at the desperate little chub. "What the whole town knows, Heston, is that you treated your uncle so poorly that he'd rather have set a match to all that money than let it go to you."

Heston shook his finger at Ian. "You know perfectly well that my uncle was a hateful, unlikable old coot, but if he'd been in his right mind, he'd never have left that money outside the family.''

"There was nothing wrong with Edwin's mind.''

"It's an old, old story,'' Heston opined. "Doddering old man, young, pretty females....''

"Oh, give it up,'' Ian scoffed. "Those three had no idea what Edwin was worth. No one did. Not even you.''

"But you did,'' Heston suggested snidely. "You knew, and I'm telling you now that I'm not about to sit by and let those women get off with my rightful inheritance. You might consider whether or not you want to do the right thing, Marshal, and back me or answer to the court why it was you let those women get their hooks in my poor uncle's pocketbook!''

An anger so hot it was cold swept through Ian. He stepped forward and stood toe-to-toe with the mayor, looking down his nose at the sweating, puffy man, his hands still riding lightly at his waist. "Are you threatening me, Heston?''

The mayor gulped but lifted his chin. Ian was well aware that the lens cap had come off the camera some moments earlier, but he was beyond caring at the moment. He leaned down, looming over the smaller man.

"Because if you are threatening me, Heston, then you'll be the one explaining himself to the courts. See, I witnessed a legal will for a man who knew exactly what he was doing and why. Edwin wanted his money to go to people who deserved it, people with good hearts, people who extended kindness and friendship to him without expecting anything in return. He did *not* want that money to go to you, because he recognized you for what you are, a selfish, grasping, lazy whiner.''

Heston gasped and reeled backward, one arm raised as if in fear. The move seemed calculated, practiced, something a sissified little boy would do when wanting to appear the victim. ''To think,'' Heston said, his chin actually quivering, ''that you would treat me this way after I got you your job.''

''You did no such thing.''

''Need I remind you, sir, that I am the mayor of this town?''

''In case you haven't noticed, Heston, you're a rubber stamp. The council runs this town. You're a glorified office manager, nothing more.''

''We'll just see about that,'' Heston blustered, drawing himself up so tight that he nearly bent over double backward. ''You'll be hearing from my attorney, all of you.'' With that he spun away, heading for his car. Silvia Chasen followed.

Brent stepped up next to Ian and muttered, ''She doesn't look much in real life like she does on TV, does she?''

Ian shook his head, but he had more important things on his mind. ''Could you hang in here a little while longer? I need to see someone. I'll make it quick.''

Brent shrugged. ''Yeah, sure. Why not? No telling who will show up next.''

Ian clapped Brent on the shoulder and started back toward his truck. He had to let Val know that the story was about to hit the national news and warn her and the others of Heston's intentions. She might not want to hear it from him, but she had to hear it from someone and soon. If it gave him one more chance to try to prove to her that she could trust him, well, what could it hurt? He didn't like how it had ended with them, and he had some understanding now of what she must have been feeling and dealing with since the reading of the will. It might even help to let her know.

Chapter Nine

Valerie stared at the sign hanging in the door window. She just didn't have the heart to open the shop by turning it around, not after a film crew had forced their way in here yesterday. But if she didn't open the shop, what else would she do? Why else was she here?

She felt lost, uncertain, adrift. Nothing about her life made sense anymore. People stared at her on the street, pointed and whispered behind their hands. Half of them probably believed that she and the others had somehow taken advantage of Edwin. The ones she didn't know were the ones who bothered her the most, however. It took some nerve to call up a total stranger and ask for money!

A tap at the door made her jump. She glanced past the sign to find Ian Keene gesturing for her to let him in. A spurt of gladness sent her up out of the styling chair and moved her feet across the floor. Tamping it down, she flipped the lock, and he opened the door to slip inside, closing it firmly and setting the lock behind him. Her happiness at seeing him again appalled her—and told her that she didn't distrust him nearly as much as she probably ought to.

"I wanted to warn you about something. We need to talk."

"Warn me?"

"I had a run-in with our good mayor a few minutes ago. He's talking to a reporter from one of those national network newsmagazines and threatening a court fight over the will."

Well, that was just the cap for her day, the national news and a court battle. And it wasn't even nine o'clock yet! She threw up both arms in a gesture of helplessness, perilously close to tears.

"He won't win," Ian promised her. "I witnessed that will myself, and so did the banker. Edwin was of sound mind. He wanted you and Avis and Sierra to have the money. There is no doubt about that."

But that wouldn't stop Heston from bad-mouthing them on the national news. The very thought was more than Valerie could face at the moment. She'd spent two days trying to convince Dillon that this money did not mean he shouldn't be applying himself at college and finish his degree. They'd argued over that blasted bike, but in the end she had capitulated. Dillon was still angry, hurt deep down inside, and she didn't know how to help him heal any more than she knew how to help herself. Add to that the reporters and the gossips and the people who had come out of the woodwork to sell her things or pester her for donations or offer to ''help'' her manage her funds, and Valerie already felt completely overwhelmed. Before she knew what was happening, she was blubbering, and then she was folded against a solid chest by two long, strong arms.

''Hey. Whoa. Hang on a minute. It's nothing to cry about. It won't come to anything, I promise.''

''I know,'' she sniffed, ''but this last week has been sheer hell.''

He patted her comfortingly. ''It's been hard for you, I can see that, and I'm really sorry.''

She looked up at him. ''Last night,'' she said, ''at nearly one a.m. a man called from St. Louis. He said God had given him a message that he and I were meant to rule the world together for a million years and I should come and get him right away.''

''A million years for a million bucks?'' Ian said with a sardonic lift of his brow. ''Hey, that's a dollar a year. Not bad. Gosh, what if it was real money? Maybe you could rule for all eternity.''

Against her will, she smiled. ''Don't make fun. I had to have my phone number changed today.''

''Problem solved,'' Ian said.

She sighed, told herself to step away now, but gave in to the urge to lay her head on his shoulder. ''I wish it was that simple.''

''One step at a time, sweetheart. Just take it one step at a time. Eventually it will all sort itself out.''

''That's what I keep telling myself, but it's all so overwhelming, incomprehensible. I mean, one day I was trying to figure out which bill to pay and which to let go, and the next I'm rich! What am I going to do with all that money?''

His hands slid to her upper arms, and he held her a little away from him. ''Nothing. Not right away. Give everything time to settle down. Then you can look at it logically and take steps to secure your future and, I'm guessing, help out your mom and brother.''

She nodded. ''The problem is that no one else wants to give it time. People are throwing credit at me like confetti, and not just me.''

''I saw the motorcycle.''

Valerie closed her eyes. ''I've been worried sick that he's going to wrap himself around some telephone pole somewhere.''

''You can't control what someone else may or may not do, Val. Just keep your wits about you so you can deal with whatever comes.''

She finally broke away from him. ''You make it sound so simple.'' She folded her arms, turning a gaze around the shabby little shop. ''Maybe I ought to go ahead and fix this place up, expand.''

''Why not?'' he said. ''Provided you don't go overboard. Frankly, I don't think there's enough hair in this town to justify adding more than a couple chairs.''

Valerie made a face. ''To tell you the truth, Puma Springs already has all the beauty shops it needs.''

''There's always Fort Worth,'' he pointed out. ''You could open a really fine shop there, and the commute's not too bad.''

''If I'd wanted to commute to and from Fort Worth

every day, I'd have set up shop there to begin with," she told him petulantly.

"So don't do anything for now," he said, the very voice of reason, "or just get in another stylist to help out."

She bit her lip. "Yeah, I could do that, I guess, take some time for myself."

Holding her by the shoulders, he told her seriously, "You don't have to live hand-to-mouth anymore. You can afford to take all the time you need."

"To think," she said, shaking her head, "that a couple weeks ago I was so desperate for cash that I feared moving my hot water heater would put me under."

"Are you ever going to forgive me for that?" he asked ruefully.

She looked up into those bright blue eyes and felt a jolt of awareness that went straight to her toes. It wasn't a matter of forgiveness. It was a matter of trust. Could she trust Ian Keene? All she knew for sure was that she wanted to trust him.

"That depends," she said, suddenly breathless, "are you going to try to convince me to?"

"Oh, yes."

He pulled her nearer, and his mouth swooped down to cover hers. For a long while, he held her there, suspended between his hands and his kiss, while the world slowed to a lazy swirl. She closed her eyes and sank into it, deeper and deeper, until that kiss surrounded and contained her, a warm, comfortable cocoon. Then he stepped close, and his arms slid around her, fitting her body to his. The cocoon began to unravel as he bent her head back with the force of his passion, and suddenly the world spun completely out of control.

She clamped her hands over the tops of his shoulders and pushed up on her tiptoes to give him greater access to her mouth. His long arms looped against the small of her back, his big hands pressing between her shoulder blades and cupping her bottom. It was maddeningly insufficient. She wanted to pull his hair and shout at him, demand more, everything.

Abruptly, he stepped back and shoved her away at the same time. They stared at one another, chests heaving, eyes wide. He sucked in air and jammed a hand through his hair. Wariness grew between them. Valerie didn't know whether to laugh or cry. She only knew that she and Ian Keene weren't finished, after all. She gulped down a lump in her throat, watched him thumb away moisture at the corner of his mouth.

"Sorry. I can't seem to be around you without wanting to do that, which, by the way, is the only reason I asked you out. I'm not after your money, Val."

"Just my body, huh?"

His mouth quirked up. "I wouldn't say 'just,' but yeah, something like that."

Folding her arms, she demanded sulkily, "So, are you going to ask me out again or not?"

He quelled a deep chuckle, and cleared his throat. "It seems I am. Are you going to agree to go out with me again?"

Valerie shrugged and looked away so he couldn't see the smile lurking about her mouth. "That depends. With the whole town's attention focused on the inheritance just now, I don't imagine we'd have much fun around here.''

"So what do you suggest?"

She tried not to be too quick about it. "We could go into Fort Worth, I guess."

He nodded, and a smile broke across his face. "I wouldn't mind seeing some of my old stomping grounds again."

"Really? What old stomping grounds would those be?"

"You forget that I grew up in Fort Worth. My parents still own a house there. I lived in it until I came here. They can't seem to decide what to do with the house now."

"Why not sell it if you aren't going to live there?" she asked idly.

"Oh, I don't know. Sentiment, I guess. We'll probably rent it out eventually. It's mostly empty now. I left just enough there to spend the occasional night. Thought it might be easier to fix up the place that way."

She nodded, but she wasn't really following. She had something else on her mind. "Ian, I'm sorry. Everything's crazy. I—it's so hard to know who to trust."

"Yeah, I get that." ·

"It's just that we were at odds from the very beginning. My fault, I know, but then suddenly you seemed to like me."

"It wasn't sudden. Well, it was. That is, I liked

you from the beginning. You were the one who didn't like me.''

"I was worried. I was out of my mind. The bills were already piling up, and then this water heater thing hit me. It was just too much.''

He briefly pinched the bridge of his nose and admitted, "Sometimes I'm a little too zealous at my job, but it was a serious problem, and I didn't want to see you get hurt.''

"I know, but I hardly got that all straightened out in my head when Edwin died and more money than I ever dreamed existed was suddenly dumped in my lap.''

"And I knew about it,'' Ian added.

"That seemed significant.''

He heaved a sigh. "Okay. I can get with that. But we're past it now, right? I mean, your money is your money. It's got nothing to do with me. You believe that, don't you?''

"I think so.''

"You just *think* so?''

She closed her eyes. "Ian, I don't *know* anything anymore. This isn't the same world. Everything's upside down, and I'm still trying to find the floor.''

"Let me help,'' he said.

"How?''

He looked her straight in the eyes then and said softly, "We'll figure it out. You'll see.''

Valerie smiled. He was either the greatest schemer ever to draw breath or he was exactly what she needed. She just wasn't sure anymore that she really wanted to know which.

* * *

He made reservations in an upscale restaurant off Sundance Square and spent the entire meal silently marveling at the shape of her golden eyes and the way her luscious mouth formed words. It required real concentration to follow the conversation, to make the appropriate responses to her litany of the insanity of the past weeks in her life. Any other time, with any other woman, that type of talk would have turned him off. Why was it, he'd often wondered, that women hacked their problems to death with words instead of doing something about them? This night he was content merely to *watch* her talk, yet the effort to actually listen felt right.

After dinner, on pure whim they browsed through a large chain bookstore that stayed open late to accommodate the weekend crowd and discovered a mutual appetite for a good mystery. Their tastes diverged widely after that, with his running to westerns and techno-thrillers and hers to romance and sci-fi. Their preferences touched again on historicals, but his personal preference ran to the Civil War and empire-building while hers channeled into geopolitical and social customs.

As they perused the stacks together, he couldn't help being distracted by the oddest things, the curve of her neck as she bent her head over an open book, the way her hair fell across her cheek, the outline of her fingers and nails as she turned a page, the way her short, silky dress wrapped neatly about her shapely body, miraculously held in place by little more than a narrow belt.

He reveled in the intermittent flash of skin revealed

by the split in the artfully draped skirt and waited expectantly all evening for the bodice to slip. Constructed of a lightweight knit fabric in a tropical, yellow-on-white print, every part of that dress, even the short sleeves, clung to her body like paint on a living wall, with nary a gap appearing where it had not been designed to do so. Ian didn't know whether to curse or praise the designer. He only knew that book shopping was rapidly becoming an erotic sport, and he spent the balance of the evening wondering how long it might be until he could get her into bed.

Once each had stocked up on reading material, they strolled around the corner to take a look around the much-touted Bass Performance Hall, which neither of them had previously visited. On the way they stopped to listen to a street band play and decided their next outing would be to the stockyards and one of the country and western clubs there. She claimed to be quite a dancer, and he didn't doubt her. He'd never thought of himself as more than competent, but suddenly he felt sure that he could keep up with her and would enjoy trying. Then they got sidetracked by a small western art museum and spent long minutes holding hands and peering through the plate glass windows at the Remingtons and Russells. A real visit would have to be put on the agenda, and Ian took notice of the hours of operation.

The Bass was an amazing building, wrought with luxurious grace and uncompromising class, but Ian realized that he was looking at her as much as he was looking at the glorious ceiling mural and polished adornments. To his delight, she, too, sneaked peeks at him from time to time, and whenever he caught her, she smiled in a shy, almost secretive manner that made his blood heat. He decided to check the Internet for a schedule of shows and buy tickets for something romantic. It would be fun to surprise her with them, though that sort of thing took planning and time to pull off. Maybe for some special occasion?

When they got back to her apartment building, he parked and killed the engine before releasing his safety belt and stretching his long arm across the back of the bench seat. She let her own belt go and shifted slightly, looking at him. He waited, but she didn't extend the invitation for which he was hoping, so he broached the subject himself.

''Do you think it's a good idea for me to come up with you?''

She looked away, and his hopes sank. ''No. Probably not.''

He tried to quash his disappointment. ''Mind if I ask why?''

Just enough light from the parking lot and square, two-story building came through the tinted truck window to allow him to see her faint smile. ''Too soon.''

He sighed and let his hand cover her shoulder. ''Doesn't feel like it, frankly.''

''I know.''

He leaned toward her, sent his hand across her shoulder to the nape of her neck. ''Why do you suppose that is?''

She shook her head wordlessly. She'd had a lot coming at her since Edwin's death, and they both knew where they'd wind up if he climbed those stairs with her. He knew she needed, deserved, some time to come to terms with the turn her life had taken, and it irritated him that he didn't want to give it to her. He didn't quite know who he became when they were together, but he liked it. That was the crazy part. He liked it, even if he couldn't figure out why.

"I had a really good time tonight," he said softly.

"Me, too."

"Can I kiss you at least?"

"At least," she said, a tiny smile curling her lips at the corners.

He slid across the seat, settled his hands at her nape and waist. As he bent his head, she lifted her chin, and their mouths met, blended. Electricity exploded in his groin, roared up through his chest and shot straight out the top of his head. Groaning, he deepened the kiss even as he hardened his muscles to derail the impulse to crush her against himself. But she did it for him, sliding her arms up around his neck and lifting her body against him. Beyond all efforts at finesse, he rammed his tongue into her mouth and hugged her so tight that he drew her up off the seat.

The close confines of the truck frustrated his attempts to ease the now painful cramp in his groin, and his boots clumped against various obstacles as he shifted, unwilling to break the kiss despite his embarrassing clumsiness. She moved against him and somehow wound up practically on top of him. Relaxing back into the seat, he turned her slightly and pulled her onto his lap. The new position quickly revealed several advantages, he availed himself of one of them immediately by palming her left breast, encountering unexpected bounty as he did so. He knew the size and shape of that breast, had measured it with his eye on many an occasion, but the weight and firmness of it surprised him, drove him right over the edge.

He slid his hand into her bodice and cupped her through the lacy film of her bra. The nipple peaked, then elongated as he rubbed it between his forefinger and thumb. Valerie gasped and threw back her head, arching into him. Then he was folding back that amazingly springy fabric and bending his head to capture that tantalizing nubbin in his mouth. He pulled at her through the lace, readying the other breast with his hand. When he switched, sucking that second nipple into his mouth with rough urgency, she made a sound deep in the back of her throat and slid downward, rubbing her pert bottom against his erection. And then a light flashed and a car door slammed somewhere nearby.

Abruptly, Ian remembered that they were making out in his truck in the parking lot of her apartment house like a couple of hormone-crazed teenagers. Thank heaven for tinted windows, though anyone who wanted to could look in through the windshield. Mentally berating his own impetuosity, he pulled back. Her lungs were pumping like bellows, her whole body quivering. He closed his eyes against the sight of that creamy, moon-washed skin enlivened by his touch. With trembling hands, he pulled her bodice closed and laid his head in the crook of her neck.

After a long while, she slid a hand into his hair, fingers splayed, and placed a tender kiss on the top of his head. He smiled and looped his arms about her waist, suddenly content, even with the persistent hardness behind his fly.

Sometime later—he couldn't have said how long— she shifted and slid off his lap, saying, "I'd better go in."

He nodded, cupped her face in his hands and kissed her. "I'll come around and get the door for you."

She shook her head. "No, it's all right. I might be tempted to let you come upstairs after all."

"Would that be so bad?" he asked.

Her golden eyes plumbed his thoroughly before she answered, "No. It would be wonderful, and that's the problem."

He smiled, despite his disappointment. "What does that mean?"

"It means that you are far too sexy for my own good, Marshal Keene," she said brightly, reaching behind her. The door swung open at her back, and she slid effortlessly to the ground. Reaching back inside, she plucked her handbag from the floorboard and quickly backed away. "Good night, Ian," she said softly. The door closed, and she walked away.

Sighing, he slid behind the wheel and rested his hands there, watching until she had climbed the stairs and entered her apartment. Only then did he start the engine and drive himself home, torn between painful frustration and growing delight.

Chapter Ten

He told himself that he wouldn't call her too soon.
His policy was always to establish firm boundaries.
His job was his priority, and he required a certain
amount of freedom in order to do it.

She had plenty to deal with herself: family, the
shop—which she only halfheartedly maintained
lately, he noticed—her friends, especially Avis and
Sierra, attorneys, financial advisers, bankers. Edwin's
personal stuff had to be disposed of and the place put
on the market. Meanwhile, Heston continued to stir
the pot, though Valerie and the other women seemed
determined to ignore him.

Ian's instinct and experience also told him that Val
needed a certain amount of space just now, and he
was glad to give it to her, believing that it made them
a better match than he'd had any reason to believe

they might be in the beginning. Still, he couldn't seem to keep his hands off that telephone. It was only polite, after all, to thank her for a lovely evening with a short call the day after their date.

He called the next day before he remembered not to. Then for two days in a row he managed to curtail the urge—by stopping in the coffee shop when he was reasonably sure she would be there. His problem then was keeping his hands off her. The urge to touch her overwhelmed him at times. He indulged himself with the slide of a fingertip down her arm, or an occasional pat on her knee beneath the table. Finally he asked her out again, and after she'd said yes, bullied himself into a full day without contact of any sort.

He took her to the western art museum, and they fell in love together with the fine art work, especially the nighttime scenes in some of the paintings. Then they enjoyed a leisurely dinner and drove home, winding up groping one another in the front seat of his truck again. She sent him away ready to pull his hair out, and he decided then that they ought to cool it. But somehow, before he knew what was happening, they were spending practically every evening together, many of them at her mother's place, which seemed like neutral territory.

Delores Blunt was good enough to make herself scarce, turning her living room and television set over to the two of them. It was hell, trying not to jump her on her mother's broken-down old couch, but he just kept going back for more.

He didn't realize that he was planning a future of sorts for the two of them until he found himself online one day considering winter show dates and making lists of possible vacation spots they might want to visit together sometime. When what he was doing hit him, he quickly got off without making a purchase and destroyed the list, once more telling himself to slow down.

What was he doing making long-range plans? He hadn't even gotten the woman in bed yet. Besides, he was not a long-range kind of guy where romance was concerned, and well he knew it. Besides, they both had too much going on in their lives just now to be thinking about the future. Best just to enjoy the moment and let the future take care of itself. It would anyway.

Still, as they continued to see one another, he couldn't help thinking that they were turning out to be a nice fit. If he and his profession did not lend themselves to marriage, well, that could work in their favor. A woman in her position would have to be darn sure of a guy to chance it, and why should she, really?

She was a businesswoman, independently wealthy now, involved with family and friends. Why should she want to get married at this point? Already she'd displayed a pattern of sorts, hanging in with a long-term, dead-end relationship for reasons of her own. Ian felt sure, knew, that he could do better by her than Buddy Wilcox.

Yes, this could settle into something really satisfying and convenient for both of them. He only hoped that it didn't take her too long to come to that same conclusion herself, because he was getting darned tired of being turned back at her apartment door night after night. Eventually a man had to have some satisfaction—and sleep.

As tired as he was of settling for a good-night kiss that routinely boiled his eyeballs, he was more just plain old tired from the demands of his job and too many late nights. More often than not, he fell into bed exhausted, only to wake alone in the throes of some erotic dream that left him more frustrated than ever. But not frustrated enough to call a halt.

Yet.

They decided to try one of the big dance clubs. Ian suggested it, and Val sensed that it was an effort on his part to defuse what had become a sexually explosive situation. Every time they were together, this potent sexual awareness literally percolated between them until it had become essentially the focus of the whole relationship. Valerie found herself wondering if it wouldn't be wisest just to give in to it and get it out of the way, but something held her back.

Her life was just beginning to settle into some semblance of normalcy. She was finally getting a handle on her finances, understanding what she really had and what she could do with it. Now she was in the process of trying to figure out what she wanted to do with the rest of her life. It wasn't the time to be melting her brain with what she expected would be mind-bending sex.

Mostly, though, it was that she had come to understand that Ian Keene had the power to break her heart. So she kept holding him off until frustration led them to the dance floor.

The place was packed when they arrived, but Ian found them a table on a balcony overlooking the dance floor. The music wasn't live on this particular night, but Valerie didn't mind. She was here to work off some frustration, not listen to some hot Nashville act. One drink into the evening, they moved onto the dance floor.

That first dance was a learning process. By the second, they had it down. The third was a raucous two-step that sent them flying around the perimeter of the floor, swinging and turning, whirling and crossing over as if they'd been practicing together for years. When the music died away, she laughed, breathless and oddly elated. He caught her hand and pulled her from the floor back up the stairs to the table.

"That was fun." He pulled out her chair for her. "It's a lot easier with a short woman, too."

"I'm not *short,*" she said with mock defensiveness.

"Petite, then."

"I'm definitely not petite."

His gaze drifted down to her chest. "Right. Not petite. Let me rephrase. It's a lot easier dancing with a woman who's the perfect size."

"Oh, you're good," she said, wagging a finger at him. "In fact, you're downright dangerous."

He just grinned and flagged the barmaid. After the second drink, the DJ spun a slow, lazy, romantic number that sent them back out onto the floor. She laid her head against his shoulder, placed her hand in his and slipped her arm around his waist. By the time they returned to the little table upstairs, it was difficult to remember that they were in public, which was exactly why they were!

"Maybe we ought to go," he suggested silkily, his breath moist and warm in the hollow of her ear, but she knew that if she wasn't very careful they'd wind up dancing on a mattress somewhere. And then what? She was afraid to believe that he was falling in love with her, that this was more than seduction on his part.

"I think you're right," she answered carefully. "I could use a cup of coffee."

She saw the disappointment in his eyes, but he was as gracious as ever. They spent an hour at a chain coffee shop. Then he took her home. For once, by mutual, unspoken consent, they didn't drive each other insane. She just slipped off upstairs to spend the night alone, wide awake and trying to figure out what the heck was happening.

It was all so confusing. After every date she wondered if she ought to have offered to pick up some of the expense. She could afford it, after all, and Buddy had almost always expected her to pay her own way even when she couldn't afford it. Ian had never so much as hinted that she ought to contribute, however. The opportunity to suggest that she would be fine with it hadn't even come up. With Ian that awkward lag between the arrival of the bill and the bill actually being paid never materialized. Still, she wondered. Mostly she wondered if she could be falling in love, and if he could be, too.

Finally she admitted to herself that she needed to know that he wanted more from her than mere sex.

She needed to believe that he *could* love her, at least. She just didn't know how much longer she could wait to find out.

Ian felt as if he was trapped in a strangely hellish but utterly compelling kind of limbo. The fact that she now called him as often as he called her salvaged his masculine pride and, he hoped boded well. They spoke daily and saw each other almost as often. They continued to go out on dates, often at her prompting. She seemed comfortable suggesting activities and to take it for granted that he wanted to spend time with her, which he did, though it had become a form of sensual torture.

They spent a Saturday at the botanical gardens drinking in the peace and playfully reminding each other that they were in a public place. One long Sunday afternoon they went to the zoo, to steal kisses in out-of-the-way places and sometimes look at the animals. Movies offered their own diversions, few of them on the screen.

They ate picnic lunches on the floor of her shop and atop his desk at the fire station, where he looked down her blouse and she kept moving his hands. They went for drinks and played countless games of darts and pool, which she often won, and they regularly groped each other in his truck, moving ever closer to that big moment. And every night she sent him home ready to howl at the moon.

He tried not to press her, suspecting that she held him off mostly because she didn't trust herself or her own judgment. The money, while it might ultimately bring relief and even joy to her, had thus far merely complicated her life. He could wait. He didn't have much choice in the matter.

Meanwhile, Buddy Wilcox had begun to hang out around the firehouse more often, even going so far as to show up for training sessions, but the sullen, knowing manner in which he watched Ian revealed that he had heard the gossip. The fire marshal and the town's youngest millionairess were a couple. Of sorts. Ian waited for a confrontation, but it never came. If Buddy had belatedly found subtlety, however, Heston had lost his. He openly sneered at Ian whenever their paths crossed, which they did on a Friday evening in late May at a gas pump where he'd stopped to fill up the fuel tank of the truck.

"Seeing the little hairdresser again, are you, Keene? Not very smart, is she? Everyone knows you've had a vested interest in my uncle's will from the beginning. Someone should perhaps inform Miss Blunt since she can't seem to figure it out for herself."

Ian struggled to keep his cool. "Someone should perhaps inform you, Mayor Searle, that slander is still a crime in this country."

"So sue me."

"I'd really rather pound you into the pavement."

"You just try it, and I'll see you in jail. Then we'll see who sues who."

Ian made himself get into the truck and drive away. It was difficult to let the slimy money-grubber's remarks go, but Ian figured it wouldn't do Valerie any good for him to punch out the smaller, softer man, no matter how irritating he was getting to be. So he was already a roiling mass of frustration when he strolled up the walk that late May evening to meet Val at her mother's.

Delores Blunt opened the door the instant he set foot upon her porch. She was an older, plumper, less stylish, physical version of Valerie herself, but she seemed to lack the strength and vivacity that was so much a part of her daughter. Ian had seen immediately that Delores had depended heavily on Val since her husband's death. It was almost as if they had swapped family roles, for Valerie never seemed to be seeking her mother's approval, not of Ian or anything else in her life. Just the opposite, in fact. It was Delores who seemed to look to Val for direction and guidance.

Ian hadn't so much as glimpsed Dillon, who was attending summer school at a state university in Denton, north of the Metroplex area. It was just as well. Ian wasn't sure, given all he'd gleaned about that young man's activities and attitude, that he had the patience to deal with Valerie's brother just then.

Barely five minutes after he entered the house, he left it again, Valerie's hand in his. He walked her to the street and handed her up into the truck, then quickly moved around the front to take his position behind the wheel.

''I heard about a new Italian place on the west side of Fort Worth,'' he said, keying the engine to life. ''How does that sound?''

To his surprise, Val made a face. ''Didn't you once

say something about showing me your old stomping grounds?''

"Yeah, something."

"Well, what's the holdup? I've had the feeling that every place we've been together has been as new to you as to me. I want to see where you've already been, maybe get a clue about the kind of brat you were."

He chuckled, oddly pleased. "Okay. You asked for it." He looked at the stretchy, strapless, hot pink top that she wore, obviously braless, with skintight black jeans cropped at mid-calf and barely there sandals. Her nails, all twenty of them, were painted icy white, and her lipstick echoed the same color as her top. She'd pushed her hair back with a pencil thin, white plastic hair band and wore it sleekly tamed. He knew just where he was going to take her. "Hope you're up for ribs, burgers, cold beer, jukeboxes and pool tables."

"Pool tables," she said, smiling. "Sounds like my kind of place." He grinned and pulled the truck away from the curb.

"I know what you're thinking," he said, "but be forewarned. One of these days I'm going to stop letting you win."

"Letting me. Ha!"

He laughed, because the God's honest truth was that she could beat him at pool every time if she really wanted to, and he didn't mind a bit.

Valerie tugged her gaze away from Ian's thigh and looked out the window. The man certainly knew how to fill out a pair of jeans—and get into hers. It was becoming more and more difficult to fight that, especially when she didn't really want to. Valerie propped her elbow on the ledge of the window and parked her chin on the heel of her hand, watching terrain she'd memorized over the past few weeks flow by the truck and wondering why she kept dragging her feet when it came to the thing she wanted most.

Yes, she'd entertained the disheartening notion that Ian might be after her money, but deep down she'd never really believed it. In all this time of going out together, he'd never asked her for a nickel, never so much as hinted at it. They rarely even discussed the inheritance or the slow pace of the probate courts. She couldn't believe that he was lavishing all this time and seductive attention on her because of the money. Then again, she could be letting lust warp her judgment.

Good grief, when had she stopped trusting herself?

Sighing inwardly, she answered that question with as much honesty as she could muster. Edwin. Once she'd thought she knew her own world and everyone in it. That world hadn't been the easiest place to live, but it had been familiar, certain, and Edwin had been a part of it. His life had intersected hers as regularly as clockwork. She could count on him being in her chair every other Thursday morning, irritable, difficult to please, somewhat needy but much too proud to parade that fact publicly, someone to be tolerated.

That tolerance on her part had made her feel as if she was a better person than some. It had aided her patience with her brother and her financial situation.

Then Edwin was gone, and not only had a small chunk been taken out of her life, she'd suffered the shock of realizing how little she had truly known him. Or herself. Or anyone else.

Nothing was as it had been. The familiar had gone or changed, or perhaps she merely saw it through different eyes now. Suddenly her mother seemed weaker, more passive than before. Her brother's troubles felt deeper than mere immaturity, and the memory of her beloved late father had warped almost beyond recognition. In addition, she sensed that she had some culpability in Dillon's problems. Worse, even her friendships had changed, especially with Avis, Sierra and Gwyn.

It was as if the four of them had pulled back from one another, herself included, and each was privately tending her own wounds. Added to that was all the craziness that had gone on since the inheritance had been made public. The media coverage had died down in a couple weeks, but Heston had become a true pain in the butt, spewing his allegations and innuendo to anyone who would listen. All together it made a picture as confusing as the hidden design things they printed in the comics section of the newspaper.

In this mesh of overlaying and interlocking squiggles and colors, Ian's was the only truly recognizable image. His was the most trustworthy, compelling aspect of her existence just then, and he wanted her. She could feel it, sense it, taste it. She took comfort in it, held on to it like a lifeline. It was the one surety in her life just then. Yet, she couldn't quite convince herself that it was for real. How could she expect to have it all? The money was miracle enough.

Except that it wasn't, not really.

What did she risk by waffling? Ian couldn't be patient with her much longer. Why not just embrace what her life had become, or better yet, remake it into something new, perhaps even actual happiness? It was exactly what she wanted. Wasn't it worth taking a chance?

She felt the brush of his fingertips against her shoulder, and turned her gaze back to him, tingling with suddenly heightened awareness.

"You okay? You're awful quiet this evening."

She smiled and reached for his hand. "I was just thinking how right it feels to be with you."

His hand gripped hers, palm up on the narrow console between the seats, and promise flared hot and bright in his electric eyes. In a voice like rough velvet, he said, "Glad to hear it, because I feel the same way."

Suddenly she knew that she was in love with him, and in that very moment, she decided. It was time. No more dithering. Tonight, even as she explored his past, she would embrace her future, their future. She turned her gaze out the window again, feeling a certain peace even as the excitement built within her. It was time to take the next step. She was ready to gamble on having it all. She was going to take a chance on Ian Keene.

Chapter Eleven

The Fireside Den was the perfect Texas anachronism, part dance club, part grill, part sports bar, part game room. Dark-wood paneling vied with stuccoed walls, sports memorabilia with western mementos and stained glass with neon signs. Chrome bar stools upholstered in supple tanned leather flanked a massive mahogany bar, and televisions playing every conceivable sports program hung from every corner, competing with a jukebox that blared country and western music. Small tables and booths tucked into every available nook and a half-dozen scattered pool tables, a video arcade, dartboards and a decently sized dance floor combined to form a massive, rambling fun house for adults. The only thing not to be found within those rock walls was an actual fireplace.

Obviously the place owed its name to its site, a

craggy knoll perched above a six-bay fire station on Fort Worth's northwest side. Val was not surprised to find that at least half the rowdy crowd wore Fort Worth Fire Department uniforms, with a smattering of police in the mix. Valerie and Ian had just grabbed one of the small tables when the greetings began. Before Val knew what was happening, they were surrounded by back-slapping men and curious women.

"Hey, buddy, long time no see."

"How's small town living?"

"Ready to get back on the roll, man? We've missed you around here."

"Life can't be too bad in the boonies," said one, acknowledging Val with a nod and a grin.

Ian made a blanket introduction. "Hey, everyone this is Valerie Blunt."

"Hi, Val."

"Nice to meet you."

"Don't believe anything this big guy tells you."

"That's right. You want the real poop, you come see me," one muscle-bound fellow said.

"Or me," his date added with a blunt stare at Ian. She was a willowy blonde with waist-length hair, tank top and shorts that barely covered the cheeks of her rump. Valerie disliked her on sight.

As if sensing trouble brewing, the muscular man extracted his arm from the blonde's grip and turned her by the shoulders toward the bar, saying, "We're dry here. See you later."

"Maybe you want to try your hands at the pool tables," the blonde suggested over one shoulder.

"Chuck and me, we're the couples champs around here. How about a game?"

Ian shook his head. "You don't want to play against us."

Stopping in her tracks, she retorted, "You could make a game of it when you wanted to."

Ian lifted a hand to the back of his neck. "I'm a fairly indifferent player," he admitted, "but I've learned a thing or two lately." He pointed at Valerie and said with a grin, "She's a damned shark. Keeps me on my game."

"And I don't like to lose," Valerie added, holding his gaze.

He laughed. "As if that was going to happen."

Fairly sure they were on the same wavelength, Valerie relaxed and reached for her chair. "In that case, thanks but no thanks on the game." Ian stepped around the table and finished pulling out the chair for her.

The blonde opened her mouth, but her date pushed her firmly toward the bar, saying to Ian, "Good to see you, man."

"You, too, Chuck. Listen, send over a waitress, would you?"

"Sure thing."

The others drifted back to their own groups and activities with smiles and winks and nods. Ian took his own seat opposite Valerie and folded his arms across the top of the table. Smiling, he began to speak, but she beat him to it.

"Old lover?" she asked with a glance in the blonde's direction.

"Old one-night stand," he answered bluntly. "That's what happens when you get too plastered to think."

"That's what happens when *you* get too plastered to think."

He grinned at that. "No one-night stands in your playbook, huh?"

"No, my poor judgment tends to be sporadic but quite long-lived."

He reached across the table and covered her hand with his. Heat radiated up her arm. "Good."

The waitress appeared. Thirty-something with a ponytail and a tiny bar apron over skintight jeans and a spandex top, she barely glanced at them. "Hi, Ian. What can I get you?"

"Hey, Shirl. Beer for me, and you can get Valerie here a frozen margarita. We'll be wanting dinner, too." The waitress nodded at Valerie and handed over menus printed on cards that she plucked from her apron pocket. Ian pushed his aside, saying, "I'll have the ribs."

Valerie took a little more time to choose the grilled chicken barbecue sandwich and avocado salad. As soon as the waitress walked away, a tall, thin, hawkish man pulled up a chair and sat down uninvited. Grinning broadly, Ian grabbed his hand in a hearty shake.

"Hey, boss!"

"That's captain to you, deserter. Or should I say marshal? How're you doing?"

"Can't complain. Let me introduce my girlfriend,

Valerie Blunt. Honey, this is Buck Dooley. Used to work for him.''

Girlfriend. The air flew out of Valerie's lungs. She covered it with a light laugh and smile. Girlfriend. Before she could decide how she felt about that assignment, whether it was too much or too little, she had to muster a greeting. "Hello."

"Nice to meet you. Best damned fireman I ever saw right here," Buck told her proudly, pounding Ian on the shoulder. "More commendations than any man in my squad. Losing him was a helluva blow, but I always knew he'd be going places." He cocked his head, straight brows suddenly drawing together. "Valerie Blunt. That name sounds familiar. What do you do, Valerie?"

"She's a hairdresser," Ian answered for her, darting a glance in her direction. "Has her own shop down in Puma Springs."

The captain nodded and dropped it. Talk turned immediately to Ian's work. They were discussing the advantages of the simpler mechanics on the older engines when a familiar-looking cop walked up.

"You son of a gun," he said, interrupting, "why didn't you tell me you were coming home?"

Ian shot a wary glance at Valerie and got up to sling an arm around the other man. They were almost the same height and build, had the same vibrant blue eyes and thick, black hair, though this man's was buzzed so short that his scalp was visible.

The captain scrambled to his feet, saying, "Don't let me get in the way of a family reunion. Good to see you, Ian." He bent forward and offered his hand to Valerie. "Privilege to meet you, Valerie. I've never met a girlfriend of Ian's before." He didn't quite shake her hand, just held it. Then with a meaningful wink, he left them.

Valerie looked up to find the policeman—he had to be Ian's brother—staring at her. Ian cleared his throat.

"Val, this is Warren," he said, dropping down into his chair again.

She offered her hand, the same hand that the captain had pressed so briefly. "Hello. Valerie Blunt."

Warren Keene lifted one booted foot to the seat of the chair that the captain had vacated and leaned forward, left forearm draped across his knee as he took Valerie's hand in his right. "Well, I'll be hanged."

"Shortly, if you don't behave yourself," Ian warned.

Unfazed, Warren whipped his gaze on to his older brother. "You found you a woman."

Valerie slid a look at Ian, who set his jaw and explained tautly, "My family have a rather unusual interest in my love life."

"Yeah," Warren quipped, "like we're interested to know you actually have one. About freaking time, if you ask me."

"Which no one did, not that it'll stop you from mouthing off."

"She's not your usual sort," Warren said, smiling down at Valerie. "Darn pretty, though."

"Thank you," Valerie muttered, wondering just what Ian's usual "sort" might be. Blond and willowy, no doubt.

"What was the name again?" Warren asked.

"Valerie Blunt," Ian answered impatiently.

Warren furrowed his brow. "Sounds familiar. Have I heard that before?"

Val looked at Ian, who quipped flatly, "Yeah, just now." He tapped his temple and said to Valerie, "Short-term memory problem."

Ignoring Ian, Warren stepped over the chair and sat down, folding his forearms against the edge of the table. "How'd you get him back here?" he ask Valerie.

She lifted her brows. "I asked."

Warren grinned broadly at that. "Yeah? We've been asking him to come home for a month."

"I've been busy," Ian grumbled.

Warren draped an arm over the back of his chair and studied Valerie with undisguised intensity. "I can see that." He sat forward again. "So," he asked Val eagerly, "ever been married?"

Valerie blinked on a gasp and burbled, "No."

"Warren!" Ian scolded.

"Thinking about it?"

"That's enough," Ian barked. "Sheesh, don't you ever let up?"

"Just because you had a bad experience first time out of the gate doesn't mean you quit the race," Warren lectured.

Valerie's interested gaze switched to Ian's face, which had gone hard as stone.

"Cool it, Warren."

As usual, Warren ignored him, saying to Valerie, "Whatever he's told you about his first marriage, it all boils down to this. They weren't right for each other.''

Valerie felt as if her chair had been yanked from beneath her. "You were married?"

Warren reared back. "Oops. Jumped the fence, I see."

"Don't you always?" Ian snapped.

Warren leaned toward Val. "Listen. Don't hold it against him. He's a good guy. The right woman could do wonders with him. Trust me on this."

"Oh, for pity's sake." Ian said, passing a hand across his eyes.

"Honestly," Warren was saying. "He'd make a great husband for the right woman."

"Shut up!" Ian ordered hotly.

"Natural father," Warren went on as if Ian hadn't even spoken. "My kid sure adores him."

Ian jumped up. "And you wonder why I don't come home more often!" He looked at Valerie, exasperation and apology crowding his face. "I'm getting our food to go." Shaking his head, he stomped off toward the bar. "I knew this was a bad idea."

Warren just shrugged. "Sensitive. Always has been. Shelly says he just can't admit that he chose badly the first time around. You know what I'm saying?"

Val sucked a deep breath, trying to clear her mind. "Shelly?"

"My wife. She's a PO. You gotta meet her."

"A PO?"

"Parole officer. Used to be a cop on the beat, but when she got pregnant with our Amber, she switched.

You gotta meet her, too, cutest little four-year-old in the whole world, our Amber. Anyway, she wanted off the street if she was going to be a mother—Shelly, I mean—and I agreed one hundred percent. Because that's how we do things in our marriage, see? We talk it out, make mutual decisions, and we support one another all the way. That was Ian's mistake. They didn't try to come to any sort of agreement. They just each did their own thing, you know, not like a real marriage at all.''

''Are you through humiliating me?'' Ian growled, showing up just then with two rigid foam containers. He reached for Valerie's hand. ''Let's get out of here before my little brother loses his head. Literally.''

She let him pull her up, mind swirling, and managed a limp smile for Warren. ''Uh, nice to meet you.''

Warren beamed as if he hadn't just been insulted and dismissed, not to mention threatened, by his older brother. ''Yeah, nice to meet you, too, Val, real nice.'' As Ian pulled her away, Warren called out to her, ''We got to get you together with my girls real soon. Okay?''

''Uh. Sure.''

''Goodbye, Warren!'' Ian said loudly, shouldering his way through the door.

Valerie waved uncertainly at a grinning Warren just before the door closed behind her. Out on the sidewalk, Ian literally propelled her along, the two white to-go containers stacked atop the upturned palm of one large hand. Valerie could feel him seething.

She was feeling a little exercised herself, but hers was more confusion and wariness.

"Okay," she said. "That was interesting."

Ian's free hand left the small of her back and clamped around her arm, drawing her to an abrupt halt. "I'm sorry," he said with heartfelt sincerity.

"You should have told me about her," Valerie whispered.

Ian's eyebrows lifted. "Oh, her," he said, "my ex. I—I guess I should have, yeah. It's just...well, I didn't think about it. I mean, I hardly ever think about her at all. Do you get what I'm saying?"

Valerie frowned. "I'm not sure. She's your *ex-wife*."

His face scrunched together then cleared. "Look, you're bound to have had boyfriends besides Buddy."

"Well, yeah. A few. I went steady with one guy for two years."

"And do you still think about him?"

"Not really. Every once in a while, maybe."

"Okay, there you go."

"But it's not the same thing," she insisted. "You were *married*."

He jerked his head. "If you say so. Couldn't prove it by me. I don't think she'd agree it was a real marriage, either. In fact, she said it *wasn't* a real marriage. When she was walking out the door, as I recall."

"So the breakup was her idea."

"Yeah, I guess you could say that."

"I'm sorry."

He made a dismissive face. "You know, it wasn't that big of a deal, really."

''Oh, really?'' she echoed doubtfully. ''Well, tell me, what did you do after she left you?''

He shrugged. ''Went to work. I was pulling a double shift for a buddy whose kid's baseball team made the finals.''

''You just…went to work?''

''My work is important,'' he said defensively. ''What else was I going to do? Ditch the shift, go cry into a beer?''

She took that in, then turned and began to stroll pensively down the street with him to the parking area. Okay, so maybe it hadn't been such a big deal, but that carried its own set of problems in and of itself. While she pondered that, he walked beside her in silence, carrying their dinner. When they reached the truck, he dug his keys out of his pocket with one hand while continuing to balance the dinner containers on the palm of the other.

He was unlocking the door when she said, ''So if you didn't love her—and you apparently didn't—why did you marry her?''

He looked down at his boots, then at the key in his hand and finally at her face. ''Guess I figured it was the thing to do. My family's big on marriage. As my mouthy little brother made obvious. We'd been seeing each other for nearly a year, seemed compatible. I mean, she was everything I wanted. I certainly couldn't find anything *wrong* with her. She thought it was time. Once I said okay, it just sort of took on a life of its own, that whole wedding thing. She seemed happy. I was fine with it.'' He shrugged. ''It should've worked out.''

"Oh, yeah," Val said wryly, opening the door. She climbed into the truck. "You had all the ingredients for a soufflé, all right. Pity you didn't have the slightest notion what to do with them or, apparently, even the inclination to find out."

She pulled the door closed and left him standing there with a puzzled look on his face. After a moment he walked around to the driver's side, handed in the food and got behind the wheel. "I don't get the metaphor," he admitted.

"It's simple," she said. "To get a soufflé, you have to want a soufflé. Otherwise, all you've got is ingredients. I mean, you can't expect them to measure themselves out, mix themselves up and jump into the oven all on their own, not that it's that easy, mind you."

"Well, there you go," he said, starting the vehicle moving. "I'm no cook."

"It's a learned skill," she informed him archly, "and like any learned skill, you have to have the desire to learn first."

"Sweetheart," he told her, "even if I wanted soufflé bad enough to try to learn to cook it, all I'd wind up with in the end would be a mess. Trust me on this."

She chuckled. "Okay. Bad metaphor. But the premise is the same."

"If you say so."

"Think chili or something."

"I might be able to work with that one, unless you've got some sports analogies."

She laughed, but then she shook her head. "I just can't believe you didn't tell me."

"Honestly, Val," he said apologetically, "it never even occurred to me. I suppose it should have, but with the new job and...hellfire, Val, this thing with you is a whole new experience for me. I—it's unfamiliar territory. I'm constantly trying to figure out where the hell I am. Except when I'm actually with you. Then I can't think of anything *but* you. It's maddening. It's—"

She reached across the truck, clamped his head in both her hands and yanked his mouth down to hers. He'd said all the right things and made her believe them. Just as they settled into the kiss, coming together over the food containers, his arms sliding around her, his cell phone rang. When he was out of town, the phone substituted for that constantly crackling radio of his. Pulling back, Ian growled deep in his throat and snatched the thing off his belt.

"No," he snarled, and to her surprise shut the thing off. He tossed it onto the seat, declaring, "Not tonight. They can damned well survive without me for one flipping night."

Valerie smiled and sank back into her seat. "Well, now that we've gotten that out of the way, can we please go someplace private?"

He looked at her, a question in his eyes that she answered with her own. They were on the move almost before she could get her belt buckled. His big hands tightened convulsively on the steering wheel, and he shifted repeatedly in his seat as he guided the truck down the hill and began turning corners.

"We're obviously not headed back to Puma Springs," she said after a moment.

He slid her a smile unlike anything she'd ever seen, an oh-baby-wait-until-I-get-my-hands-on-you promise that curled her toes.

"Much closer than that."

She nodded, not trusting herself to speak without purring. A feral, palpable heat filled the truck cab. Valerie felt her body softening, swelling, sensitizing.

This night, she knew, was going to change both their lives.

Chapter Twelve

Ian turned the truck into a narrow drive and parked it in front of an old-fashioned, one-piece garage door. The small frame garage stood detached from the small frame house. A neat, white box with dark green shutters, door and roof, it sported a ledged, red brick veneer about waist high and a covered porch some six-feet square that protruded beyond the front door. A row of low, dense shrubs lined the entire front of the house and the narrow walk that led to the street.

"Welcome to the Keene house," Ian said, shutting off the engine.

"This is where you grew up?"

He nodded. "My parents deeded it to my brother and me when they moved to Lubbock. I lived here until I moved to Puma Springs."

"And now? You'd said something about renting."

He lifted both hands in a gesture of puzzlement. "Yes, we've talked about leasing it out. Warren and Shelly have their own place, a lot nicer and larger than this. But nothing's been decided. I think they're hoping I'll move back in eventually, but I don't think I ever will. Meanwhile, I keep a few things here in case I need or want to spend the night."

Spend the night. Valerie's heart thudded and sped up. Striving for nonchalance, she lifted the food containers. "I hope there's something to eat on."

"Yeah," he said, "if you don't mind basic. I mean, very basic."

"I don't mind," she told him, a little breathless, "but we'd better get at it before the food's stone cold."

He lifted the forefinger of his right hand as he opened the truck door with his left. "Microwave," he said, smiling broadly, and got out.

He escorted her to the side door stoop as if navigating a minefield, watching where she put her feet and steering her with the light pressure of his hand at the small of her back. A light with a motion detector sensor came on as they climbed the steps. He had the door open in a blink. The flick of a switch illuminated the tiny utility room through which they passed to reach the kitchen. Had the washer and dryer for which it was prepared been in place, there would have been just enough room to walk between them without banging elbows.

The kitchen was a long narrow space with built-in appliances, including a microwave above the stove, cabinets painted a pale yellow and a dining area at one end. A card table and single folding chair occupied that space, and Valerie carried the food containers to it. Ian opened the shutters above the bar that separated the kitchen from the living area, letting light into that space before walking into it to retrieve one of a pair of webbed lawn chairs, which he positioned at the table in the dining area. A lopsided recliner, a wobbly three-legged occasional table and several packing crates comprised the remainder of the visible furnishings.

It was stifling inside. Ian switched on the air unit in the window in the end of the dining area, then went into the kitchen to take forks and knives from a drawer. He picked up a roll of paper towels from the white tile countertop and placed these on the card table, along with salt and pepper shakers. "I should've picked up something to drink. All I've got here is water and beer."

"Water's fine."

Ian clumped back into the kitchen and opened a cabinet. "Um, beer would be better. Forgot to run the dishwasher. No clean glasses."

Valerie smiled to herself. "Okay." She tore off paper towels and folded them, then arranged the flatware next to the food containers while he fetched beer from the refrigerator, returning to the table with two frosty bottles.

"Need to reheat anything?"

Watching the steam rise from his potato, she shook her head. He placed the beer on the table and pulled out the folding chair for her.

"It's not the Ritz," he said, "but it's private."

Then, just as she stepped up to the chair, he pulled it out of the way and slid his arms around her, adding, "Which means I can do this."

Bending his head, he kissed her with measured thoroughness. At first, he merely pressed his lips to hers, but then he adjusted the fit and began a long, thrilling process that required nibbles and licks and hard, slanting pressure. By the time he slipped his tongue into her mouth, she was weak in the knees and clinging to him, her arms twined about his neck. He explored and tasted, stroked and plunged, and all the while his arms folded her tighter, plastering her body to his from hip to chest until finally his hands wandered down to her bottom, cupped her and pulled her higher. At the same time, he pushed his knee between her thighs. Valerie shuddered as she rode against him, astounded at the level of stimulation.

Her head began to spin. The darkness behind her eyelids deepened and intensified. Gradually, she realized that he was pulling back. Slowly but surely he disengaged, reversing his slow process until finally he lifted his mouth from hers and, with a groan, pulled her head down onto his chest, cradling her gently against him.

She could feel the thrum of his pulse and knew that he was fighting to control his breathing. Closing her eyes, she savored the intimacy, the simple need to feel him there in that place with her.

After an extended moment, she tilted her face up, smiled and said, "It may not be the Ritz, but the service is top rate."

He chuckled and teased, "I hope you're contemplating an appropriate gratuity."

She told him with her eyes exactly what gratuity she was contemplating, but pulled away languorously, saying, "Let's just wait and see if the food meets the standard."

He brought the chair around for her, and as she sank into it murmured against her temple, "I can promise that dessert will meet all expectations."

"No dessert until you eat your dinner," she said primly, but her heart was already pounding again.

He sat down in the lawn chair, and they began to eat. She enjoyed the very tasty sandwich while watching him tuck into the ribs, stripping the bones clean. They made a messy meal, but as he tore more paper towels from the roll and mopped up his face and hands, he said, "This arrangement has lots of pluses, you know. Here I can eat like the slob that I am."

"Ah-ha, so it comes out." She waved a hand airily. "This is all so you can pig out without embarrassing yourself."

He crooked an eyebrow and smiled, and just like that she was all but panting again. She forced her attention back to the more easily satisfied appetite. They ate in near silence afterward. She managed about two-thirds of the sandwich, then pulled out the filling with her fingers and ate that, leaving the remainder of the bread. Ian, meanwhile, polished off the ribs and dug into the potato. Replete, Valerie sat back and watched him consume the baked potato, skin and all. When it was done, he reached for a piece of her leftover bread and began mopping up the sauce and melted butter in the bottom of his container.

Valerie just shook her head and took another look around her. "So," she began, "how long did you live here?"

"From about fourth grade until I went off to college. I spent a couple summers here, more or less. You know how it is. Then when Dad retired and he and Mom relocated to Lubbock, I moved back in and took over the place. They didn't want to sell or rent, and it didn't make sense to let it sit here empty. I'm not sure what's going to happen with it now, but I'm leaning toward selling it myself."

"Did you live here with *her?*"

He looked up sharply. "Mary Beth?"

"If that's your ex-wife's name."

He dropped the bit of bread left and picked up a paper towel to wipe his fingers before sitting back in his chair and answering warily, "Yeah."

"Then she would be responsible for the decorating."

He shrugged. "What about it?"

She studied the lattice-print wallpaper above the painted wainscoting, the verdigris light fixture above the table, the clean tile countertops and white appliances.

"Not bad," she decided, realizing the potential. He just nodded. She sat forward, folded her arms against the edge of the flimsy table and said, "Tell me about her."

He blinked and shifted his weight. "She was, er, is, about five-six, slender, long hair."

"Blond," she guessed.

"Blue eyes," he went on, confirming her assumption. He tapped his chin and said, "She has a little cleft right here and a birthmark on her elbow."

"But what about her as a person?"

He sucked in a deep breath, obviously thinking. "She's nice, not too emotional. I mean, not the shrieking sort, which I appreciated. She likes her sisters and shopping and rock music." He shook his head and said, "It wasn't her. I know that. I've heard that she's married again and expecting a kid. We don't hate each other or anything like that."

Valerie nodded, pleased. They'd have had to share a stronger emotion than she suspected they had in order to hate one another now. Still, something bothered her about all this. He could have been describing the woman back at the bar instead of his ex-wife, at least when it came to the general physical characteristics.

"So why me?" she heard herself asking. "I don't seem to be your type."

He linked his fingers together, rested his hands atop the table and admitted almost conversationally, "I don't know. I just know that I get something by being with you that I've never gotten with anyone else. And that if I don't make love to you—soon—I'm going to go stark raving mad."

Valerie's heart stopped, but a moment later it began beating with a smooth, strong, invigorating rhythm that filled her with a surge of purpose. She rose calmly to her feet and lightly said, "Well, we can't have that."

He looked up at her, his fingers tightening, shoulders stiff. "Can't have what? Me going crazy or the two of us finally making it to bed?"

She bent over, brought her mouth close to his and whispered, "Oh, I think Puma Springs is entitled to the sanest of fire marshals."

He got up, shoving his chair all the way back to the wall behind him, and cupped her face in his big hands. "You blow me away, do you know that? You absolutely blow me away."

Her heart was pounding and her breasts felt so full that they hurt. "I'm in love with you, Ian," she told him. "You must understand that."

He shoved the table out of the way and swept her up into his arms. "I think I must be in love with you, too," he said roughly, carrying her out of the room. "I sure can't find any other name to put to it, and believe me, I've tried."

She put her head back with a sigh and closed her eyes, feeling her body wafting through space in his strong arms. She had thought money was the root of her problems and that Edwin's bequest would be the cure for the dissatisfaction that had ruled her life, but now she knew how wrong she had been. It came to her, there in the enveloping darkness of Ian's boyhood home, that Edwin had always known what really mattered. He hadn't cared a thing about the money he had amassed. All that had mattered to him were those he'd loved. Loving and being loved were true wealth. Finally, finally, she understood his true legacy.

"I didn't plan this," he told her, his voice a velvet

caress in the near-total darkness, "which is not to say that I haven't been thinking about it, hoping for it."

"I've been thinking about it, too," she whispered into his ear, and his chest puffed out on a quickly indrawn breath.

He carried her lightly down a narrow hallway that opened off the front end of the living room before turning left and stepping into the darkened bedroom. Pausing, he dipped and straightened again, hitting the light switch with his elbow. A lamp came on, revealing the simple, full-size bed bereft of both head and footboard. He felt a moment of doubt.

The yellow blanket that lay folded across the smooth white sheets and the single pillow resting against the light gray wall at the head of the bed seemed woefully shabby. An ugly lamp stood next to the bed atop a small, square table that he'd covered with a faded red towel to hide the cracking finish and reduce the need for dusting. He'd always like the clean gray walls and shiny white woodwork, which he'd painted to match the vinyl miniblinds covering the single window, but the place suddenly seemed utilitarian and cold to him now. Even the two doors that stood open in the wall opposite the bed, one leading to the tiny bathroom and the other to the tinier closet, seemed somehow inadequate.

"It's not much," he said, setting her on her feet. "I'll understand if—"

She turned and leaned into him, looping her arms about his neck. "Make love to me, Ian."

He closed his eyes and bowed his forehead to hers, his hands lightly grasping her waist. Then he tilted his head and covered her mouth with heady urgency, pulling her hard against him. She went up on tiptoe, plastering her body to his, her flat belly cradling the long, hard ridge behind the zipper of his jeans. He plumbed her mouth with his tongue and slid one hand up to cup her breast. Her nipples peaked and something clenched deep in the pit of his belly. She seemed almost to swell against his hand, and he moaned impatiently, his fingers tightening around her breast.

It was not enough. Pulling back, he folded down her strapless, elasticized top with both hands, freeing her breasts. Perfect. Utterly perfect. He stared at the smooth, full globes with their tightly peaked, rose-pink nipples and felt his erection buck. Reaching up, he carefully covered both luscious mounds with his hands. She jerked and moved her head back.

"Beautiful," he murmured, awed by this unexpected bounty. "I didn't realize...." His gaze switched to her face. "You're beautiful," he told her. "Perfect." He shook his head. Why hadn't he realized what he had here?

Tears gathered in her eyes, and alarm spurted through him, but then she smiled, hooked her thumbs in the elasticized top folded about her waist and began working it down over her hips. He watched, mesmerized by the way her breasts swayed slightly like ripe, succulent fruit when she bent at the waist. He swallowed, mouth watering as she stepped out of her sandals and kicked away the confining twist of her top. He rocked back, heart pounding like a jackhammer, when her hands went to the waistband of her capris.

She broke the snap and slid the zipper down. A single shove sent them to the floor, and she stood before him in black bikini panties. Oh, man. He stared for a long while, his gaze sweeping up and down her body repeatedly. If that was not womanhood in all its glory, he didn't know what was. He couldn't wait to get his hands on her.

Tugging his shirttail free, he peeled the neat, knit polo over his head and tossed it away. She stepped forward, lifted one hand and smoothed it over his chest from shoulder to shoulder and down to the waistband of his jeans. He closed his eyes and tried to concentrate on breathing as her hand lightly stroked him. When her fingertips slid beneath his waistband, he convulsed, and his eyes popped open.

She smiled up at him through the long, black thicket of her lashes and lifted both hands to slide them slowly from the center of his chest and down his ribs to his hips, where she paused, lightly pressing both thumbs into his navel. He thought his knees would buckle. As if sensing that might be the case, she leaned into him and undid his belt. He couldn't bear any more.

Taking over, he swiftly ripped the belt from its loop and dropped it before opening his fly. He wrapped his arms around her, felt the rapid draw of her breath and smiled with satisfaction. He began walking her backward toward the bed, his knee moving between her legs, his gaze holding hers captive. When she reached the side of the mattress, he swept her up into his arms once more and placed her in the center of the bed, her head upon the pillow. Then he sat down next to her and yanked off his boots and socks.

He kept his pants on, knowing that if he stripped now, he'd be inside her way too soon. He wanted her insane first, wanted this first time imprinted indelibly on her brain. Crawling up onto the bed, he straddled her and sat back on his heels, lightly stroking her body with his fingertips from shoulders to mid-thigh. Her skin went from cool to hot as he repeated the process, trailing up and over the firm mounds of her breasts, down her slender torso, across her quivering belly and past the creases at the tops of her thighs. The third time, he caught the narrow elastic band of her panties and peeled them down her legs, sliding backward with them until he stepped off the end of the bed and could ease them over her feet and drop them to the floor.

Sweet, merciful heaven. That was the very essence of womanhood reclining there upon his pitiful little bed, one knee slightly bent, one hand spread across her belly. He wanted to howl and beat his chest. Better yet, he wanted her to howl.

Slowly, he crawled forward, once more straddling her with his knees, until he could lean down and kiss her. He filled his hands with her breasts, gently fondling as he took her mouth again and again. She moved restlessly beneath him, clamping and unclamping her thighs. He smiled inwardly and concentrated on making her feel every stroke of his hands and tongue to her core.

When she was panting and rising to meet his touch,

he shifted to one side, sliding his mouth along the curve of her jaw to her throat and downward. Traveling lower, he licked and sucked, nipped and tasted, while his hands feathered down her body until they reached the apex of her thighs. He cupped her, feeling her body's moistness against his palm, before carefully inserting a finger.

She shuddered and spread her legs for him. He became lost in her body's response, which became more and more animated as he stroked her. Her climax came swiftly and was almost violent in its intensity. Humbled and proud in the same instant, he knew that he had never seen anything more beautiful, and he told her so, his heart squeezing inside his chest.

It was almost as if she took him there with her, as if he actually glimpsed that one place of personal pleasure deep inside where no else could ever really go. He felt overwhelming joy. He wanted to give her that, wanted to share it with her until they were both completely drained of energy and every molecule was replete with satisfaction.

Something told him that if he could manage that she would be his, really his. He might not be good husband material, but he could be the finest, most selfless lover she had ever known. It wouldn't matter that he could never be like Warren, that he was too self-centered and focused, too dedicated to his job. He could give her such pleasure that the rest of it wouldn't even register. He could make her happy. This way, he could make them both happy. All night long. Maybe even indefinitely.

Chapter Thirteen

He spoke to her; she knew he spoke to her, but the actual words escaped her. She escaped herself, falling away in a delirious rapture, until nothing was left but the swirling tingle in her nerve endings.

She could not say how long it went on. She seemed to spend a lifetime tumbling and whirling and tumbling again, almost floating down to earth only to find herself falling from some new and unexpected precipice into a fresh tide of euphoria, until finally she went away from herself completely.

She drifted, until she slowly came to herself again and gradually developed an awareness of where she was. Reclining on her side, she lay cuddled against his chest, his long, strong arms wrapped around her as he rocked her gently side to side. After a time she became aware of the hard length of his erection between them and realized with a jolt that they had really only just begun. Oh, my. Again.

Smiling and stretching like a cat, she slid her arms up around his neck and lifted her mouth to the underside of his chin. In a twinkling she was on her back again, and he was looming over her, pressing his pelvis to hers. She slid her hands down his flanks and got another jolt when she realized that he was still wearing his jeans. Struggling up onto her elbows, she glared at him.

"What are you doing still dressed?"

He looked down at himself ruefully. "Hardly dressed."

"Overdressed, if you ask me."

"Easily fixed." He shoved off the bed and onto his feet in one smooth, powerful movement. Shucking his jeans, he suddenly looked up at her. "Birth control," he said succinctly.

Valerie gave her head a slight shake. "I—I never had much reason to use it."

He leaned down and kissed her. "I'll be right back." With that he swiftly moved toward the door on the left.

Val lifted her eyebrows, enjoying the sight of his broad shoulders, tapering torso, long, muscular limbs and tight tush until he disappeared from view. A light came on in what was obviously a small bathroom. Hugging several new revelations to herself, Valerie rolled onto her side and propped her head on the heel of one hand. Her body still pulsed, heavy in places, liquid in others. All in all, she felt sleek and supremely feminine. Her mind had never seemed so clear, her body so energized and so relaxed at the same time. She could hardly wait for the rest. Smiling to herself, she thought how amazing the evening had thus far been.

Ian returned moments later, tossing a handful of foil packets onto the bedside table. "They're old, but I didn't find any expiration date," he said, his hands on his hips as he looked down at her.

Valerie delighted unabashedly in the view. He was beautifully made and seemed even larger without clothes. His firm, solid body showed surprisingly little hair, except in the groin area. Her eyes widened at the proud display there, but she did her best to remain nonchalant. Reaching languidly for one of the small, shiny squares piled on the bedside table, she looked at it and turned the packet over in her hand before tearing the foil with her teeth. He pounced, literally, pinning her to the bed, inky hair falling forward over his forehead as he stretched out atop her, glorious in all that bare, male skin.

"Do you have any idea how much I want you?" he asked huskily, sliding his long body against her.

She reached down with one hand. "Oh, a very large idea."

He laughed. Then his mouth swooped down to capture hers. He pushed between her legs and settled himself heavily into the V of her thighs. His clever hands sought her breasts as his tongue pierced her mouth. She was panting and writhing against him before he rose up on his knees, found the torn packet that she had dropped mindlessly, and sheathed himself. Then he lifted her knees with his hands, positioned himself between them and pushed into her with one long, smooth stroke.

She felt utterly filled, complete, and she hovered there, impaled by him and suspended between that now-familiar euphoria and a supremely luxuriant lethargy, until he began to move in long, purposeful thrusts. She lay back, smiling, her gaze locked with his as passion built. She felt his tension and his leashed power as he moved against her, inside her. Slowly, purposefully, he drove her to the very edge of rapture. They danced there, surging and undulating against one another.

Each lunge heightened her arousal and pushed her closer to fulfillment and further from herself, but this time, when that moment of utter separation of self came, it had evolved into a joining with him so complete that she could no longer feel her body, her soul, apart from his. They spiraled together, exploding in a frenzy of sensation that blew away everything else. Thought, speech, even sentience in its strictest sense, left her. Or perhaps she abandoned them, willingly, gladly giving herself up to a tidal wave of hedonism, happily drowning in it.

Later she once more found herself on her side, her back to his chest, slick now with perspiration, his arms about her. She sighed, utterly replete. So this was making love. It seemed unreal, fantastic, mythical. She closed her eyes and drifted on a cloud of dreamy contentment, wafting toward sleep and expecting that he was doing the same. But then he pushed his knee between hers and his hand slid over her hip and downward. She caught her breath as his hand slipped between her legs. Desire pulsed through her again, faster and stronger than before, roaring to life in an instant.

"Do you know how many ways there are to make love?" he asked, his voice a rough, hot whisper against her ear. She barely managed to shake her head. "Let's find out."

Valerie stretched, arms lifting above her head, toes pointing, back arching. As sleep left her, awareness crept in. She recognized the heaviness at her back just as a long, strong arm coiled about her shoulder and angled downward across her chest. The events of the previous night rushed back to her, and she felt a corresponding sensitivity and plumpness between her legs. Smiling, she eased onto her back and opened her eyes, looking straight into Ian's blue ones. There were worlds in those fascinating blue orbs, new, exciting, welcoming worlds. It was like coming home to a place where she hadn't even known she belonged.

"Morning, beautiful."

"Mmm." She snuggled closer, head pillowed on his upper arm, cheek pressed to his chest as he lay stretched out on his side. "You're nice to wake up to."

"I was just thinking the same thing about you."

She looked up at him through her lashes. He needed a shave. The blue-black shadow of his beard darkened his jaws, chin and upper lip. A lock of ebony hair fell forward rakishly over one eyebrow. He looked devastatingly handsome. If she hadn't fallen for him already, she would have done so in that moment.

"You're very cheerfully attractive in the morning."

"I am this morning, cheerful, that is." He kissed her forehead. "Sleep well?"

"Very, but I'm not surprised. How late was it when we finally turned off the light?"

"Past four."

"Good grief."

His hand cupped her breast, and he nuzzled her ear with his nose, murmuring, "I didn't hear any complaints at the time."

"You aren't hearing any now, either."

"In that case," he said, bringing his mouth to hers even as he turned her onto her side and pulled her leg up over his hip.

She laughed. The man was delightfully insatiable, and so, she had discovered, was she.

Perhaps an hour later, she stood beneath the spray in his shower, letting the hot water beat the soreness from her limbs, when he called through the door, "Take anything in your coffee?"

Coffee. Just the word tasted of ambrosia on her tongue.

"Nope. I like it black and strong," she told him.

The door opened slightly, and he reached inside, placing a steaming cup on the narrow counter beside the sink. The welcome, heady aroma of rich, freshly brewed coffee permeated even the steam of the shower. "My hero!" she exclaimed, quickly shutting off the water.

The bathroom door opened fully just as she stepped out of the tiled cubicle. He leaned a shoulder against the door frame, wearing nothing more than his jeans, and watched avidly over the rim of his coffee cup as she reached for a towel with one hand and her own cup with the other. Giggling self-consciously, she clutched the towel beneath her arms and sent him a wry look before sipping the fragrant black coffee. Putting her head back, she let the hot brew slide down her throat.

"Mmm." She slid him an arch look. "I think I'll keep you."

Chuckling, he set his cup down where he'd previously placed hers and sauntered over to slide his hand beneath her towel. "I think I'll let you. Figuratively speaking, of course."

She tilted her head and tried to ignore the heat pooling in her groin as his hand shaped her breast. "Does the money bother you?"

He targeted her face with a frank gaze. "Why should it? Your money has nothing to do with me."

"It doesn't bother you that I have so much more than you now?"

He narrowed his eyes in silent admonition. "My ego is not that tender. I have my work, which is very important. Your money, frankly, means nothing to me. Period."

She smiled, believing every word. "I knew there was another reason I loved you."

"Another?" he teased, and one brow arched knowingly. She stretched up on tiptoe to bring her mouth to his in a coffee-flavored kiss. A door slammed, and Ian's head jerked up. "Damn! He wouldn't."

"Ian?" a familiar voice called, and Ian grimaced.

"Warren. Blast his hide!"

"I'd better get dressed," she said, setting her coffee cup next to his and bending her head in order to towel her hair.

"I'll try to get rid of him," Ian promised, sweeping out of the room. She heard him stomping into his boots.

"Ian?" The voice was feminine this time.

"Shelly? Uh. Just a minute. Be right there."

Valerie heard him muttering under his breath as he left the room. She wondered what to do. Should she stay hidden, hope they'd go away soon? Safely wrapped in a towel, she stuck her head out of the bathroom, found the bedroom door closed and hurried to locate and don her clothing. She'd left her handbag, with the few cosmetics she carried, in the kitchen, so she simply availed herself of the spare toothbrush Ian kept in the bathroom for himself and tousled her wet hair with her fingers. After that, she paced the bedroom, trying to decide what to do. Stay hidden or meet the family?

Staying hidden seemed ludicrous, but meeting the family under these circumstances could be very awkward. She cooled her heels a while longer, listening to the murmur of conversation. She began to wish that Ian would take the decision out of her hands, that he would come for her, proudly introduce her to his sister-in-law. Then the voices in the next room grew louder.

"That's none of your business!" she heard Ian snap.

"All we're saying is that if she's here, Shelly would like to meet her." Val recognized Warren's voice.

She bit her lip even as Ian retorted, "Maybe she doesn't want to meet Shelly." Well, that would never do. She couldn't have Ian's family thinking that she was unfriendly or standoffish.

Returning to the small bathroom, she took another look at herself in the mirror. The strapless top seemed oddly risqué for the daytime, especially with this morning's freshly scrubbed appearance. She tousled her hair with her fingers again, pulling and plucking until she was satisfied that she could manage no better styling. Moving back into the bedroom, she headed for the door, then impulsively detoured to the closet. She found a single pair of jeans with a torn hem and three button-up shirts. Choosing a soft, faded chambray, she slipped it on over the strapless top, turned up the collar, rolled up the sleeves and tied the tail snugly at her waist. Certain that it was the best she could do for now and remembering how many times Ian had told her that she was beautiful, she went out into the hallway.

Though not as loud, the conversation taking place in the living room was clearly audible from the hall, and Valerie paused to gauge the mood before revealing herself.

"We don't mean to butt in," said a woman's voice. "It's just that we're so glad you've finally found someone, and we did wait until after noon to drop by.''

Valerie smiled.

''Thank you,'' Ian said, ''but why can't you just wait 'til we ask you instead of barging in uninvited?''

''Because you're liable to have her married before it occurs to you to introduce her to the family,'' Warren answered flippantly.

''No one's even mentioned marriage but you,'' Ian barked, and a warning tingle ran down Valerie's spine. It was true that the subject of marriage hadn't come up exactly, but it eventually would. Wouldn't it?

''Why not?'' that very soft, very feminine voice was asking. ''Isn't she the sort of girl you'd consider marrying?''

''Of course, she is,'' Ian said quickly. ''Val's great, and I'm crazy about her. If I was willing to try marriage again, it would be with her.''

If he was willing?

''But you're not,'' Warren stated, his voice rich with disappointment and tinged with disgust. Valerie closed her eyes, her stomach sinking. ''I can't believe you haven't gotten over the divorce.''

''You know that's not the case,'' Ian said.

''Then I really don't understand it, Ian.''

''Look,'' Ian said with obvious exasperation. ''I don't *want* to be married. I'm no good at it.''

Valerie covered her mouth with her hand and leaned into the wall.

''It wouldn't be fair to her anyway,'' he went on. ''My work's too dangerous.''

"No more dangerous than mine," Warren pointed out.

"But Shelly knows the score," Ian argued. "She was on the street herself. She knew what she was getting into from the beginning."

"And you think Val doesn't understand about your occupation?" his brother asked.

"I don't know," Ian admitted, "and it doesn't matter. What makes Val perfect for me is that she doesn't *need* a husband."

"That doesn't mean she doesn't *want* a husband," said the female, Shelly.

"Val's not like that," Ian insisted. "She was with her last boyfriend, I don't know, years."

Valerie folded her arms across her middle, feeling physically ill. Did Ian really think that what she'd shared with him resembled in any way the on-again, off-again, almost-but-not-quite-official relationship she'd had with Buddy?

"She's pretty young, yet," Warren was commenting doubtfully.

"Twenty-four," Ian confirmed, "but what neither of you realize is that she's independently wealthy. She inherited a large sum of money and, if she's in the least sensible, ought to be set up for life. I meant it when I said she doesn't need a husband."

"So you're just two consenting adults in an uncommitted relationship?" asked Shelly.

Valerie bowed her head, waiting for Ian's answer. After a long moment he said somewhat offhandedly, "Yeah, pretty much."

Two consenting adults in an uncommitted relationship. Valerie felt as if the rug had just been pulled out from under her. She literally stumbled backward and wound up sagging against the wall. Last night obviously had meant nothing to him. She closed her eyes, beating back the agony of disappointment.

What a fool she was. She had convinced herself that the money didn't matter to Ian, and it didn't, not the money itself. No, what mattered to Ian was the freedom that her wealth brought him. He would never have to take care of her, never have to consider her welfare, never have to commit himself, so even if she wasn't particularly his type, well, at least he would never have to marry her.

For a moment, the pain of that realization threatened to engulf her completely. She could not catch a breath, could not see, could not hear above the distant buzzing in her ears. Gradually, the miasma passed, leaving behind a deep, sharp disillusionment. All that remained was to face it down and get out of there.

She pulled the shreds of her pride around her and pushed away from the wall. Then, after fortifying herself with a deep breath, she walked around the corner into the living room, not really sure what she intended.

"You're wrong," Ian was saying, though in response to what, Valerie didn't know. "Maybe most women are that way, but Valerie doesn't need a man. Believe me, even without the money she's quite capable of fending for herself."

"You're absolutely right," Valerie agreed, and Ian swung around as all eyes targeted her. She parked her hands at her hips and the words just fell out of her mouth, unplanned, unrehearsed, blatant. "I mean, really, a woman with money just needs a man for one thing, and that happens to be the one thing that Ian is really good at."

The shock that swept the room was palpable. Both Ian and Warren were standing, with Ian nearest her and Warren, who seemed younger and slighter than last night in jeans and a sport shirt, standing next to the rickety recliner where his wife, a compact brunette with a short, sleek haircut and big brown eyes, sat in khaki shorts and a tank top. Valerie found that she couldn't look either Warren or his wife in the eyes, so she looked to Ian instead.

"Valerie," he said hesitantly. "We, uh, we were just talking about—"

"Marriage," she interrupted, "yes, I know. I hope you told them how ridiculous that would be."

"Ridiculous?" Ian echoed uncertainly.

She shrugged, "Of course. Why would I marry now? Someday if I do choose to marry it would have to be to someone completely capable of pulling his own weight."

Ian slowly tilted his head. "You aren't, of course, implying that I couldn't."

"Outside of the bedroom, you mean?"

The brunette gasped, but the anger that flared in Ian's eyes gave immediate satisfaction.

"That was uncalled for."

"Was it?"

Warren's wife, Shelly, came immediately to her feet, saying, "We shouldn't have come here."

"No, you shouldn't have," Ian agreed, turning his anger on them.

Warren stepped up behind her. "We just wanted to lend a little support."

"I know what you wanted," Ian retorted. "You just wanted to twist my arm, see to it that I do what *you* think I should. Well, thanks a hell of a lot."

"Oh, that's right," Valerie snapped, "how dare they care about you? How dare anyone care about you?"

"That's not what this is about!"

"Of course not. Stupid me. You're the one who always knows best. We established that early on, didn't we?"

Ian's mouth dropped open. "That again! You would've preferred that I let the damned hot water heater blow you to bits?"

"I would have preferred," Valerie said coldly, "that I never laid eyes on you."

Ian froze, and for a long moment, no one said a word. Then Shelly laid a hand on her husband's arm, a look of sympathy in her gaze for Valerie.

"We should be going."

Warren nodded morosely. "Ian, I'm sorry. This was my fault."

"I'm well aware of that," Ian snapped, but then he turned away and slid a resentful glare at Valerie. As if he had reason to be resentful! "Maybe it's for the best."

"Maybe it is," Valerie said. Warren cast a doubtful, apologetic glance her way. She tossed her head, arms crossed, unwilling to like him or his brother any longer. Head hanging, Warren followed his wife toward the door.

"We meant to help," Shelly said over her shoulder, and Val realized that the woman was talking to her. The look of apology, of understanding, in her eyes nearly undid Val.

She lifted her chin. "You did. Just not the way you meant to maybe."

Shelly looked at Ian and shook her head before walking out the door in front of her husband. For several moments after the door closed behind them, Ian kept his back to her. Then he abruptly turned and said, "So I guess I dreamed it all?"

Valerie felt a fresh stab of pain. "Evidently we were both dreaming."

He stared at her, then finally asked, "What now?"

She looked away from him. "Now I want to go home."

"And that's it?"

She wanted to ask what else could be when love obviously meant one thing to him and another to her, but her throat felt clogged with cotton, so she simply nodded.

He brought his hands to his hips and bowed his head. "Well, if you can handle that, I guess I can, too." He lifted a hand, indicating that she should precede him to the door.

Valerie kept her shoulders back and her head high as she walked out of the house, but a hole had opened in the middle of her chest, and something told her then she was never going to find a way to fill it again.

Chapter Fourteen

Valerie pulled the paper toward her, ink pen in hand, and looked up at her brother, who sat next to her before the attorney's desk.

"You understand the terms? The income is substantial but not great, and you can't touch the principal until you're twenty-five."

"I understand."

"Once I do this, Dillon, you're on your own. No bailouts, no loans, no monetary gifts of any kind."

"I understand, Sis, and I won't disappoint you, I swear."

"And you'll stay in school?"

"Absolutely. I've already made arrangements to pay next semester's tuition."

"Okay." Valerie smiled and signed the paper before passing it to Dillon on her right. "You're going to do just fine."

"I'll do better than fine," he said confidently, signing his name.

The attorney handed her another paper, and she signed that one, too, before passing it on to her mother, who sat on her left. "Your turn."

"Really, Val," Delores Blunt said, scrawling her own name on the form, "you didn't have to do this."

"I know, Mama," Valerie told her, sitting back with a keen sense of satisfaction, "but it's best this way. Now I don't have to worry about either of you."

Delores put down the pen and laid her hand over her daughter's wrist. "I wish I could say the same about you."

Valerie patted the plump, loving hand. "I'm fine, Mama. Really I am." And she was, at least as fine as she could be. "It's just been a very confusing time, that's all."

Delores nodded. "I know. It seems so strange to have money. I—I'm almost afraid to believe it." With a sudden frown, Delores turned to Corbett Johnson, the attorney, asking, "What about Heston Witt? He keeps saying he's going to contest the will."

The attorney smiled ruefully and shook his head. "I'm sure he'll try, if he can find an attorney foolish enough to attempt it on percentage, but I assure you, the will is ironclad, and while plenty of attorneys might be willing to fight it, they wouldn't do so without a hefty retainer up-front because winning isn't likely. I don't see Heston coming up with that kind of money. In any event, I don't think we have anything to worry about legally, but that's not to say that Heston isn't vindictive enough to stir up trouble where he can.''

"I'm developing a thick skin where Heston is concerned," Valerie commented dryly.

"That's good," Corbett said, "but if he crosses the line, we can always sue for slander."

"We'll keep that in mind," Dillon told him, rising to his feet, "but personally I'd like to rearrange his face for him."

"You will do no such thing," his mother admonished, also standing.

"I only said I'd like to, not that I was going to."

"See there. He's already showing signs of imminent maturity," Valerie quipped, rising to dispense hugs as her mother and brother departed.

She signed a few more papers having to do with her own remaining funds and investments, then she thanked Corbett, whose assistance had proven invaluable, and made her way down to the street below. Feeling a small surge of pleasure at the sight of the sleek, red coupe parked at the curb, Val dug out her keys, depressed the electronic key button and got in behind the wheel.

It wasn't the most prestigious model on the market, just a reliable, midpriced two-door with a sporty look and a few amenities, but it was paid for, fully insured and dent-free. Now she was in the market for the right property, a lot close to town where she could build a small house for herself. So far she hadn't seen the right spot, but she was in no hurry. No hurry at all.

Life in the last week or so had slowed to a crawl,

and she couldn't seem to find the energy to pick up the pace. She spent long hours just sitting and staring into space, her mind a sluggish blank, and if she tried to bully herself into making decisions and setting plans into motion, she'd only run out of steam in a matter of hours or even minutes. If she stopped moving, it was a real struggle to get going again, so she wasted no time starting up the car and backing it out of the space.

It was only as she drove down the street that she realized she didn't have anyplace to go. She'd learned to keep her distance from most people since the inheritance, having learned quickly that envy did strange, often ugly things to some of them. As for her so-called friends, the party would always be at her expense now, and in most of their minds she was no longer allowed to have problems or complaints. Anything that bothered her was seen as petty and treated with a certain amount of hostility because she had money now, and they wanted, needed, to believe that money solved all problems.

Since Edwin's personal effects had been disposed of, even she and the other heiresses had drifted apart, each consumed with her own life. She'd been the first to pull away. She'd hardly seen Avis and Sierra since she'd started dating.... No, she wasn't going there. Best just to concentrate on the matter at hand.

It was too early for lunch, and her aerobics class didn't meet until the evening. She was sick of sitting home alone, but she was equally tired of her mother hovering and worrying that she was depressed. In the end, there was really only one place to go. She headed for the shop, where the stylist she'd hired to fill her newly installed second chair would undoubtedly have everything under control, despite the amazing increase in business lately. Still, it was safe.

It was, in fact, the one place where she could be certain that she wouldn't run into *him*.

Ian sat on the edge of the desk and glanced at his wristwatch. Four minutes past midnight. Fatigue pulled at him, but he knew that if he went home he'd just toss and turn endlessly. Usually he had some adrenaline going after fighting a fire, even a small one, but tonight he didn't even have the energy to clean up. He'd turned down the guys when they'd invited him to join them for a beer after they'd put out the small grass fire that had mobilized the unit. That was probably not a good move on his part, but he didn't feel much like keeping company.

Rubbing a hand over his grimy face, he weighed his options. He could take a run or get in a little more strength training in the back room, but he didn't have the energy for that. He could try to watch a movie on tape or make another stab at reading, or he could tackle the never-shrinking mountain of paperwork on his desk. Might as well do something useful.

He glanced at Brent, who occupied the desk chair, and said, "Why don't you take the rest of the night off? If you don't want to meet the guys for a drink, I'm sure your wife would be pleased to have you at home for one night."

"Naw, she's sleeping. No point in upsetting the schedule."

"You must be tired. Been a while since we've really had to work."

Brent leaned back in his chair, considering, and clacked his teeth together. "Anything strike you as odd about that grass fire?"

Ian shrugged. "It's been dry. I'll admit that it's fairly unusual for a blaze like that to start at night, but we'll probably find a cigarette butt or tobacco and nicotine residue at the point of origin tomorrow."

"Mmm. Probably. I was thinking more about the team, though."

Ian's gaze sharpened. "You noticed that Wilcox was right there in the thick of things, too?"

"Yeah, what's up with that? In the past, he's shown real limited interest in actually fighting fires, but tonight he was like this one-man crew. Hell, if we'd all stood back, he'd have put the thing out entirely on his own."

Ian shrugged. "Maybe the real thing showed him how important the job is."

"Or maybe he's a fire bug, the kind that gets off on the flame."

"You think we ought to keep an eye on him?"

"Can't hurt."

Ian nodded. "Okay, then." He glanced around him with a sigh. "Sure you don't want me to take over for tonight?"

Brent sat forward and propped his elbows on the edge of the desk. "What's wrong, Ian?"

"Wrong? Nothing's wrong. I'm just too keyed up to sleep. You know how it is."

"You haven't slept well in days."

Ian shrugged and waved a hand, avoiding Brent's gaze. "I keep thinking about all this paperwork. It's like rabbits, multiplying in the dark of night."

"I've never seen you like this," Brent said, completely ignoring Ian's excuse. "You seem so...unhappy."

Ian leapt off the corner of the desk. "I'm not unhappy. Why would I be unhappy? I'm just... overworked."

"Which is a good reason to go home and get some rest," Brent pointed out.

Ian sighed. "I told you, I can't sleep."

"Because you're overworked."

Seeing that he'd talked himself into a corner, Ian gave in. "Yeah, you're right. This is the last place I need to be. What I need is a cold beer and a long, hot shower."

Suddenly he flashed back to another hot, steamy shower and felt again the delightful anticipation as he waited for just the right moment to toe open the door and catch her there, gloriously nude and glistening wet, gulping back a giggle as she reached one way for a towel and the other for the coffee with which he'd tempted her. His gut twisted as the memory dissolved, and pain shot through his chest.

How had he read her so entirely wrong? She was like every other woman, after all, completely bent on marriage. Except that she wasn't like every other woman. She wasn't like *any* other woman, and he had the memories to prove it. Damn. No matter what corner he turned, he always came smack up against the same wall. She wanted marriage; he didn't. One of these days maybe he'd stop wanting her.

Then again, maybe not.

He bid a hasty farewell to Brent and went out to his truck. An hour later he'd aimlessly driven every street in Puma Springs, winding up on the one where Valerie lived. The light was on in her upstairs apartment window, and Buddy Wilcox's battered automobile was parked in the apartment lot. Sick at heart, Ian drove home and sat down with a bottle of Scotch.

"Hi."

Gwyn turned from wiping down the glass front of the bakery case and parked her hands at her slender hips, cleaning cloth and all. "Well, hello there, stranger. How're you doing these days?"

Valerie let the coffee shop door close behind her and managed a tentative smile. "Okay. How are you?"

"Just okay?" Gwyn asked, walking forward and plopping down on a stool at the end of the counter. She hung her elbows on the countertop at her back and settled in to talk.

"It's been strange," Val admitted, glancing at the table where she and the others had so often sat and visited. "Seen Avis and Sierra lately?"

Gwyn shook her head. "Sierra's leased out the flower shop so she can spend more time with her daughter, and Avis just locked the door on her place. Said it didn't make sense to invest the kind of money needed to make the changes that the fire marshal wanted. I suppose she'll eventually dispose of her in-

ventory. Speaking of our hunky fire marshal, haven't
seen him lately, either. What's he up to these days?''

Valerie dropped her gaze and walked over to strad-
dle the stool next to Gwyn. ''I wouldn't know.''

''Aren't you seeing him?''

Valerie just shook her head and changed the subject. ''You never answered my question. How are you
doing?''

Gwyn shrugged, then sighed. ''Things have been
pretty slow, if you must know. Business usually picks
up with school out, but that new drive-in hamburger
joint at the end of Main is eating my lunch just now,
so to speak.''

''What are you going to do?''

''Wait it out. Those teenagers will get tired of yelling at each other through their car windows and start
hanging out in here again. I'm updating my menu to
make it a little more teen-friendly, putting in a malt
machine, that sort of thing.''

Val felt a twinge of guilt. ''Gwyn, if you need
money, I'd be glad to make you a loan.''

Gwyn lifted a hand. ''Nope. Nope. That's the last
thing I need, another loan.''

''A gift, then.''

Gwyn folded her arms. ''No way.''

''But—''

''Listen to me,'' Gwyn interrupted, laying a hand
on Valerie's shoulder. ''When you gals first inherited
all that money, I was purely mad. Why you? Why
not me?''

''I don't know,'' Valerie whispered.

''And you know what?'' Gwyn said. ''It doesn't

matter. You hit the jackpot. I didn't. It's just that simple.''

''Nothing's simple,'' Val muttered bitterly.

''Well,'' Gwyn said, ''it is, and it isn't. Now, speaking of unanswered questions, why aren't you seeing Ian Keene? I thought you two were paired up.''

To Valerie's horror, she felt her chin begin to wobble, and the next thing she knew, she was blubbering like a kid with a skinned knee.

''Oh, honey,'' Gwyn said, wrapping her arm around Val's shoulders. ''I guess it's true. Money doesn't solve all problems. Tell me about it.''

Valerie knuckled tears from her eyes and told all.

''Now isn't that just like a man?'' Gwyn said when Val had concluded her story. ''I gotta admit, though, if my relatives ever did anything so highhanded as that to me, I'd probably do and say a lot worse.''

''It's my own fault,'' Val admitted with a sniff. ''He said he loved me, and I just assumed that meant the same thing to him that it did to me, that we had the same goals and plans. We never actually discussed it, though, and like some lovestruck adolescent, I fell right into bed with him. And I thought I was being so careful, too.''

''In my experience, kiddo, nothing lends itself less to good sense than love, but the question now is, what are you going to do?''

Valerie shook her head. ''Nothing to do.''

Gwyn inhaled deeply and said, ''You know, it's just possible that he does love you but hasn't yet come to terms with what that really means.''

Valerie sighed and said, "Maybe, but even if that's true, I doubt he'll ever come to terms with it."

"Could be," Gwyn admitted, eyes narrowing.

Valerie got up from the stool to go. "Anyway, thanks for listening."

"Anytime," Gwyn replied. "In case you haven't noticed, this is the new sweeter, gentler, more caring model of Gwyneth. All part of our new customer service plan. Spread the word, will you? I need the business."

Valerie chuckled. "I was pretty fond of the old model, too."

"I know," Gwyn said. She smiled thoughtfully as Valerie left the shop. "That's been the difference in you and me."

When the door opened to his office, the very last person whom Ian ever expected to see was Gwyneth Dunstan, but there she stood in neat, cuffed shorts, tank top, bobby socks and worn hiking boots. Her straight, biscuit-brown hair had been caught up in a no-nonsense ponytail on the back of her head, and she wore absolutely no makeup whatsoever. Gwyn was about his own age, maybe a little older, and pretty enough. He had once found her admirably fit. Now she seemed rather unattractively thin and hardened.

"I want you to understand something," she said, right off the bat. "I don't usually make it a habit to stick my nose in where it doesn't belong. Okay?"

Ian blinked and belatedly climbed to his feet. "Okay."

"That said," she went on, stepping over Cato's prone form to drop into the chair wedged in front of Ian's desk, "I think you need to know something."

Ian warily lowered himself to his chair and rocked back. "So let's hear it."

Gwyn laid one hand on top of his desk and said bluntly, "You're breaking Valerie's heart."

Ian rocked forward again, swamped with unwelcome emotion: anger, embarrassment, resentment, even a dash of hope. Quickly squelching the latter, he frowned at his visitor. "You're right. You're sticking your nose in where it doesn't belong."

"I don't deny it, but somebody's got to do something. I've never seen Val like this. Even when she was worried sick about paying her bills and her little brother flunking out of college, she always had that light in her eye. Laughter was always percolating just beneath the surface, a good time waiting to happen. Now all she seems capable of doing is beating herself up and missing you."

Ian fought down twin surges of elation and guilt. She wasn't missing him, he told himself. She was missing whatever goofy fairy-tale ending she'd dreamed up for the two of them. He knew too well that fairy-tale endings were not real. Running a hand over his face, he tried to concentrate on the other things Gwyn had said.

"Valerie has no reason to beat herself up."

"Yeah, well, the way she sees it, she held on to her heart all these years and then gave it away for nothing."

He winced at that. "We both made a mistake. It wasn't just her."

"No kidding," was Gwyn's acerbic reply. "But I have to wonder, was the mistake getting together in the first place or breaking up?"

"Look," Ian said impatiently, cutting to the chase, "I don't know what she told you, but here's the abridged version. She obviously wants to get married. I don't. Been there, done that, failed miserably at it."

"Well, get in the pity line, cowboy, just understand that it's a real long one. About half the people who've tried their hand at wedded bliss are in it, including me. The other half, I hear tell, go out and find someone who'll hang in and fight whatever problems come along. Valerie strikes me as the fighting kind."

"Maybe Valerie is," Ian conceded, gut knotting. "I'm not."

Gwyn sat back and folded her arms. "So the big, bad fireman is a coward at heart. Who'd have guessed?"

Ian ground his back teeth together. "I didn't say that."

"Sure you did."

He brought his hand down on the desk hard enough that Cato threw his head up in alarm. "Don't you understand? Valerie deserves more than I can give her."

Gwyn rose slowly to her feet and leaned forward slightly, keeping her face level with his. "Oh, really? Or is it the other way around now that she's got all that money tied up good and tight?"

Ian was on his feet in a heartbeat. "I'm going to forget that you said that."

"Smarts, does it? Maybe that's the problem. Maybe you're afraid that some people will think you're with her for the money."

"I don't care what some people think," he insisted, but even as he said it, he knew that it wasn't completely true. He just hadn't admitted to himself that his pride could take a beating if everyone believed he was after her money, and why wouldn't they? Even Val had believed it at first.

"So all you're afraid of is failure," Gwyn pressed. "You've learned nothing from past mistakes."

"I've learned my limitations," he snapped.

"You mean that you've learned not to try," she said, bringing her hands to her hips. "You didn't learn that fighting fire, I'll warrant."

He rocked back on his heels, blindsided by that. "It's because I fight fire that I'm not... I can't be what she needs."

"Right," she said disdainfully. "Fighting fire's like the priesthood, I guess. No, I forgot. No vow of celibacy."

Now that was plain hitting below the belt. "I think you've said enough."

She ignored him. Straightening, she mused, "I'm really surprised by all this. I thought Val, at least, was too smart to get mixed-up with a poser like you. At least she's done the smart thing with her money, set up trusts for her family and herself. I only hope Avis and Sierra are as wise about their inheritances—and wiser about their men."

"We can hope," Ian sniped, but then he folded his arms, determined to get back a little of his own. "Tell me something, Gwyn. How much of this is you trying to stay on the money side yourself? Aren't you just a shade jealous of your friends' good fortune?"

"Oh, yeah," she admitted bluntly. "If you really want to know, I was mad as hell at first. Why them and not me? But then I thought about it, and I finally had to admit that they deserve it and I don't. They genuinely cared about that old man. Me, I've been too mad at the world to really care about anyone or anything but my kids in a long, long time, and to tell you the truth, I'm not absolutely certain that I've cared about *them* as I should have. I'm working on it, though, and I figure that's more than you can say."

Ian blinked at that. Then he gulped. Was it cowardice that kept him from trying again with Val? Or was failure just a convenient excuse not to care? But he did care, more than he wanted to, and the awful truth was that he couldn't remember ever feeling about Mary Beth the way that he felt about Valerie. Still, if he should fail again... Maybe he was a coward. Gwyn certainly thought so.

She stepped over Cato on her way to the door, saying, "If you have a brain in your head, Ian Keene, you'll sweep that little gal off her feet and right into church before some other lucky guy manages it, because you can bet they're beating a path to her door and some of them won't care so much as they're able to pretend. Normally, I wouldn't worry about her, but she's vulnerable now, thanks to you."

Ian couldn't stop himself from asking, "Is she seeing someone else?"

Gwyn turned with her hand on the door knob. A grin darted across her face. "Not that I know of. But I hear Buddy's been after her lately, and he's not the only one. They aren't lining up six deep to get their hair cut just because the moon's full, you know. Maybe you ought to think about that." She pulled open the door, turned through it and pulled it closed behind her in one fluid movement.

Ian absently dropped back into his chair, with an unpleasant image nagging at him, a line of men snaking out of Valerie's shop and around the corner to the street. They were all bearing gifts, and they all looked just like Buddy Wilcox.

Chapter Fifteen

Half past ten at night and it was hot enough to steam water. Storms had blown through the area earlier, and now the air felt muggy and thick. Summer had descended with a vengeance, as it was apt to do in Texas. After three busy days of thunderstorms, tornado warnings and high winds, they'd enjoyed one truly beautiful sparkler, temperatures in the upper seventies, sunshine and calm, blue skies. Then abruptly the thermometer had climbed into the midnineties, a cooling breeze was not to be had east of the Llano Estacado and the sun had hung over the rooftops with killing concentration. Now, even with the sun hidden away for a two good hours, it felt as if someone had left the oven on, which at least partially accounted for the slow pace of Ian's steps as he followed his big, black dog along the sidewalk, heading home after an evening stroll.

He walked with his head down, his hands tucked into the pockets of his jeans. Cato, too, was drooping, tongue lolling out the side of his mouth, head and tail practically dragging on the ground. The walk had done neither of them any good. Ian felt no closer to sleep, and Cato was certainly no cooler than before they'd set out. Maybe a cold shower would help.

As if eager for that dreamed-of shower, Cato suddenly lifted his head and took off at a dead run. Ian sighed disgustedly and picked up his pace, calling the big brute to heel. The dog ignored him, and when it bounded across the yard of Valerie's mother's house, Ian instinctively knew why. Cato didn't so much as pause before leaping up the steps and disappearing into the black shadows of the porch. Ian's own footsteps slowed, but he wasn't about to walk on by. He'd secretly been hoping for this for days. In many ways, it had been inevitable that he would meet Val here.

Heart pounding, he climbed the steps and moved into the shadows of that darkened porch. Damn, Gwyn was right. He was a coward. Otherwise he'd have gone looking for Val days ago.

She sat in the center of the bench swing at one end of the long, narrow structure, her legs, arms and feet bare. Her hair had been pulled back from her forehead and fixed with some sort of clasp, but the night shadows withheld all other details from him. Cato had parked in front her, and she concentrated on ruffling his big head with her hands as she crooned a private greeting. Ian did not doubt, however, that she was as fully aware of him as he was of her.

After a few minutes, she gave Cato's broad head one final pat and sat back. Satisfied, the dog rose to all fours, circled and lay down on the cool planks of the porch floor. Ian took a deep breath and found his voice.

"Mind if I sit?"

She shrugged and slid to one end of the swing. The clump of his boots sounded absurdly loud to Ian as he walked over, turned and eased himself down beside her. She sighed and lifted a hand to her head but didn't speak. Even after all this time, he wasn't sure what to say himself, so he used his legs to set the swing into gentle motion. She pulled her feet up and tucked them beneath her.

They sat there, swinging to and fro for a long time. The night finally began to cool. An odd sense of comfort, of calm settled around them, and Ian silently acknowledged the first moment of peace that he'd felt in nearly three weeks.

Suddenly he heard himself saying, "God, I've missed you."

Her feet hit the floor, but she didn't bolt as he expected. He licked his lips and tried again.

"Val, I'm sorry. I know I blew it. I—I assumed things. I held back things. I was so fixated on my need to make love to you that I didn't... I was *afraid* to discuss the future with you, afraid it would derail us, and then I did that anyway. I've been kicking myself for it because I need to be with you. Right here, right now, anytime, anywhere, I need to be with you.''

For a long, terrifying moment, she just sat there, and then, to his immense relief, she scooted toward him. Tentatively, he held out an arm, and she settled against his side, resting her head in the hollow of his shoulder. She pulled her feet up again, and he looped his arms around as much of her as he could embrace, holding her tight.

''I've missed you, too,'' she whispered, turning her face up.

He could no more have stopped the kiss that he dropped on her mouth then than he could have stopped the moon from rising, and once he'd begun, he couldn't seem to do anything but kiss her for a very long time. Strangely enough, it wasn't a particularly sexual thing. He knew at the very heart of his being that she wasn't about to slip off to bed with him again, not now, not yet, and that was okay. It wasn't about sex, well, not *just* sex, not anymore. He lifted his head finally, and for the first time in days he felt as if he could actually breathe.

''Gwyn came to see me,'' he said.

She looked around at that. ''Gwyn?''

''Yeah. She really busted my chops, and I won't say she was right about everything, but she made some sense.''

''She's the sensible type. What'd she say?''

''Doesn't matter. I just thought you should know that she cares enough about you to stick her nose into something that isn't really any of her business.''

Valerie chuckled. "Really ticked you off, did she?"

"Oh, yeah, but she was right enough that I got over it. Her heart's in the right place, anyway. She says you've taken care of your inheritance real well. I was glad to hear that."

"I've always been the sensible sort, too. Of course, until now I never really had a choice."

"Sure you did," he told her softly. "You didn't have to step up to the plate and help your mom keep it together after your dad died. You didn't have to open your own shop and work day and night to keep it afloat, to pay your brother's tuition."

Valerie shrugged. "Yeah, well, Mom doesn't need my help anymore, and neither does Dillon, thanks to Edwin."

"And you."

"Setting up their trusts was the best thing that's happened out of this," she told him, "especially when it comes to Dillon. Funny, but now that I'm not riding him anymore, he's actually doing rather well."

"Nobody likes to have his hand forced," Ian said firmly, and she sensed that he was speaking of himself as much as Dillon.

"That's what Warren was trying to do that day, force your hand."

"He meant well," Ian said. "He always means well, but he can't make decisions for me, and I resent that he tries."

She nodded. "So what are you saying? That you didn't mean those things you said?"

"I meant them at the moment. Mostly."

"And now you've changed your mind?"

He couldn't lie to her. He was still agonizing over this. "I don't know. I just know that I've been terribly unhappy without you. I need you in my life, Val."

She bowed her head briefly. "What does that mean, being in your life?"

He searched for the right words, shook his head and made a stab at it. "I'm willing to explore all the possibilities, but I need time to ensure that it would be different this time, that I will do better. Can you do that, Val? Can you give me, us, some time?"

She looked at him for a long moment, then she tilted her chin and brought her mouth to his. All the tension drained out of him with that kiss. He hadn't quite blown it, after all. They hadn't tossed around any declarations of love, and that bothered him more than he'd have expected, but the important thing was that they still had a chance for something special. They broke the kiss and settled in together. He closed his eyes and held her tight, savoring the closeness.

After a while, she cleared her throat and said conversationally, "I hear you've been pretty busy at work lately."

He couldn't help wondering if she'd heard about that from Buddy, but he just shrugged. "Series of small fires, nothing much, really. The rain seems to have brought a halt to it."

"That's good."

He nodded, and she laid her head on his shoulder. He crossed his legs and closed his eyes again, relishing the moment, and the next thing he knew, he was jerking awake with a sharp intake of breath. One booted foot hit the porch deck with a loud *clump*. Valerie started at the sound and looked around, seeming confused.

"What is it?"

"Guess I dropped off. Haven't been sleeping too well lately."

She yawned, and the radio on his hip crackled.

"Repeat. Fire One, this is dispatch. Marshal, are you there?"

So that was what had awakened them. Ian straightened with a scowl, muttering, "I should've known." He grabbed the thing from his belt. "I'm here," he said into the tiny microphone. "What's up?"

"We've got a barn burning on the west edge of town," came the reply. Ian groaned and climbed to his feet as the dispatcher went on. "The Mac place, sector three, number one-four-one Jessup Street."

He keyed the radio and said, "I'm on my way. Call up the crew." Frustrated, he sent Valerie an apologetic look. "So much for the rain slowing down the fire season. Sorry, honey, but I have to go."

She slipped to the edge of the swing, her lower lip clamped between her teeth. Then she shook her head. "No, it's all right. It's your job."

"I'll call you in the morning," he promised, dropping a quick kiss on her mouth.

"Be safe," she said.

"Always," he promised, warmed by the simple admonition. He jogged down the steps. "Cato, we're up, boy."

Trotting across the yard, he headed down the sidewalk toward his house, Cato at his heels. He felt fifty pounds lighter than he had earlier that night, and he knew that it didn't have a darned thing to do with cooler temperatures or short naps. The world had righted itself again. He felt in control of his life again. Content with that, he turned his mind to his job.

Valerie sat there in the dark watching him disappear into the shadows beneath the trees while the past lonely weeks without him rose up and smacked her right in her face. Was she insane to let him back into her life? They hadn't settled anything. The future remained as uncertain as ever, but she couldn't deny that she felt oddly empowered by the knowledge that he had missed her as much as she missed him. She believed that Ian cared about her, but did he really love her? Did he love her enough to commit to spending the rest of his life with her? And if he didn't, then what? She wasn't sure that she had the strength to walk away from him again. She could hardly bear to let him leave to do his job.

What if something happened to him tonight, just when they were beginning again, just when they'd promised one another a chance?

A chill swept through her, and for the first time, she understood how hard it could be to sit around and wait to hear that he was all right after fighting a fire. But who said she had to sit around and wait?

Ian might be a little upset that she'd followed him, but he couldn't do anything to stop her, and he might as well understand now that he'd have to make some concessions if they were to build a life together. Maybe she didn't have the right to ask him not to risk his life, but neither did he have the right to ask her to sit by while he did it.

She got up and went into the house for her shoes and purse.

Ian trudged back to the truck, weighted down with heavy protective gear. In one hand he carried a shovel and in the other, a handheld radio. He'd pushed his broad-billed hard hat to the back of his head and smeared soot across his face when wiping away the sweat. Grimy, smoky and hot, he nevertheless felt a deep, abiding sense of satisfaction and not a little surprise. He was in for another when he saw Valerie standing patiently beside his truck.

"Don't be mad," she said, dropping the arms she'd held folded across her middle. "I was just curious."

He sent her a doubtful look, knowing perfectly well that she was here out of concern more than any curiosity, but he let it pass, rather pleased.

"I'm not mad. "He tossed the shovel into the bed of the truck and sent the hat after it before dropping the radio onto the seat through the open window. "Curiosity seekers can be a big problem for fire fighters, but I don't think you fit that category. If this had been a bad one, though, the site would have been cordoned off. This one was mostly smoke. Some old crankcase oil somehow spilled onto some rags and hay and lumber. As it was, we got it under control pretty quickly and saved the structure itself. Thanks to a friend of yours."

"Oh? Who would that be?"

Holding her gaze with his, he said carefully, "Buddy was the first one on the scene."

"Buddy Wilcox?"

Ian grinned, relief sweeping through him at the surprised, doubtful tone of her voice. "Yeah, Buddy Wilcox, and I have to say, he did a pretty good job of securing the site and containing the fire until help got here."

Valerie lifted an eyebrow. "I'd have bet money that Buddy would be the last on the scene, not the first. He talks a big game, but you have to pretty much take that stuff with a grain of salt."

"Yeah, I know what you mean," Ian said. "In the past, I noticed a pronounced tendency to do as little as possible on Buddy's part, but he seems to have had a change of heart lately. Every time we have a fire event, Buddy's there."

"I guess stranger things have happened," Val muttered skeptically.

Ian chuckled, but sobered, remembering. "I thought your opinion of Buddy might have changed. I, uh, saw his car parked outside your apartment real late one night."

Valerie fixed her gaze to his and said significantly, "Oh."

Ian stripped off the heavy coat that he wore over equally heavy coveralls, playing for time, but in the end he simply confessed, "I couldn't sleep. I've had that problem lately, and I was out driving that night." He bowed his head and scratched a spot behind his right ear, admitting, "It was probably one in the morning."

She rocked back on her heels, a small smile tightening her lips. "Yes. There was a fire that night, as I recall, and Buddy came pounding on my door, telling me how he'd put it out practically all by himself."

"Well, he made a significant contribution," Ian qualified. Then he asked the question uppermost in his mind. "Did you let him in?"

She looked him straight in the eye. "Nope. And when he showed up again later the next day, I more or less told him to get lost."

"More or less?"

She shrugged. "He was being unusually sincere, told me that he'd changed. Then he asked me out, and I told him I didn't think that was a good idea, that I wasn't ready to see anyone."

"What'd he say to that?"

"Said he was going to prove himself to me. Said he was going to make me forget you. I told him I just didn't see that happening."

Pleased, Ian smiled. "Yeah? That mean you're my girl?"

She tilted her head. "I've been unhappy without you, too, Ian."

He lifted his hands, realized how grimy they were and just let them hover about her shoulders. "We're going to work this out."

"Okay," she said, and they stood there smiling at one another like a couple of idiots for what seemed like a very long time. Finally, Val cleared her throat and grimaced. "Well, it's late."

Ian sighed. "Yeah, and I've got to clean up and

get some liquids down before I can hit the sack. At least I think I'll sleep for a change.''

"That's good," she told him softly. "I'm going now so you can do what you have to and get some rest." She turned away, but he caught her by the wrist, stopping her.

"I'll see you soon." It was as much a question as a statement.

"Whenever you like," she said, her soft, golden gaze holding his.

It was all he could do to let her go without kissing her again, but he was far too grimy and sweaty for that, so he gradually loosened his grip and let her slip away, confident that he would be with her again soon. Beyond that he dared not speculate. He had once envisioned a future of semicommitment, an exclusive sexual relationship, freedom in all else. Now the most important thing was making sure that she never left him again. He just wasn't sure how he was going to do that.

Ian laughed, his arm tightening about Val's upper chest as he pulled her more tightly against him. They sat entwined on the floor in front of the television. They'd spent every evening together for more than a week. It was simply understood now that when he wasn't working or sleeping, they'd be together. He'd stopped by her apartment around dinner time tonight with a couple burgers and cold beers in tow. She'd been listening to the weather forecast on the evening news when he arrived, and since they were still way behind on yearly rainfall, this was of particular interest to him, so she'd left the television on while they ate.

Two hours later they were caught up in a goofy sitcom neither of them had ever before watched. She laid her head back onto his shoulder and savored the chuckles that rumbled against the walls of his chest and telegraphed tremors to her spine. He seemed as happy and content as she felt; yet, the old tension simmered just beneath the surface.

Another hour passed, then the evening news came on. They checked the weather once more, confirming a forecast of dry heat followed by more dry heat. Finally Ian sighed and said, ''It's getting late. I'd better go.''

She smiled with resignation and nodded, then turned her face for a sideways kiss. His hands slid over her body, his right one covering her left breast and the other cupping her cheek and holding her head steady while his mouth negotiated the perfect fit with hers.

Memories of the night they'd made love wrapped themselves around her, bringing sensations that she'd already relived countless times. But this was real. This was now, and dear heaven, the man could kiss. He put everything he had into it, lips and teeth and tongue, even the soft caress of his breath. She twisted in his arms until she could get hers around his neck, and then he was pulling and pushing her until she was sitting on his lap facing him, her legs about his waist.

''Ah, sweetheart, it gets harder and harder to leave you,'' he said softly, and she knew that he was waiting for her invite him to stay, but the memory of the sadness following the last night they'd spent together kept the words locked behind her teeth. So instead of words, she brought her mouth to his and kissed him deeply.

He put his head back on the sofa cushion and opened for her. She stroked her tongue over the smooth, even edges of his teeth and tasted the sweet inside of his mouth, pressing herself against him as she did so. He reached between them to adjust himself, then cupped her bottom in his wide palms and pressed her against the hard ridge of his fly. Need knifed upward inside her even as molten heat flowed down, and suddenly she couldn't think of a single reason why she should deny them the satisfaction they both so obviously craved. The hand that he shoved up beneath her T-shirt did nothing to persuade her otherwise.

Rocking against him, she reached down and tugged at his belt. His hands convulsed against her back where they'd ventured in quest of her bra clasp. When she pulled the snap on his jeans, he slid down slightly and released the hook on her bra band. The garment went slack. She found the tongue on his zipper but only managed to ease it down an inch or so before he forced her arms up by shoving her shirt up over her head and off, taking the bra with it.

A new urgency gripped them both, and he arched forward, lifting her slightly and taking one peaked nipple into his mouth as she struggled with that zipper. Then he was lifting her higher and yanking at her shorts and panties while he suckled her. Gasping with alternating waves of heat and cold, she pulled up first one knee and then the other, kicking her feet free. He pulled back long enough to rip his polo shirt off over his head and shove down his jeans, reaching between her legs where she straddled him to get them as far as the tops of his thighs.

Absolutely frantic now, she reached between them, grasping his hard length, positioned him and worked herself downward. Ian threw his head back, a groan rolling up out of his chest. Then he lifted his hands to her breasts, and she began to move, rising and falling, rocking from the knees. His hands dropped down to her breasts before he lifted one knee, slid one hand down her body and slipped it between her legs.

Light exploded behind her eyes, and she instinctively increased her pace, but then he abruptly bucked upward and clamped both hands down on her hips, trapping her.

"Wait. Wait! I forgot."

She couldn't even find her tongue to ask what he was talking about, but then he reached behind him and dragged cushions off the sofa, tossing them onto the floor behind her. Wrapping his arms around her, he folded his legs back and rose up onto his knees, taking her with him. Carefully he leaned forward with her until she was on her back atop the cushions. He rested against her for a moment, and she felt him swallow before he gently lifted free of her. Rolling into a sitting position, he quickly yanked off his boots and socks before sliding his jeans down his legs. Then he upended the jeans and shook out the contents of his pockets. Plucking a foil packet from the coins, keys, pocketknife, wallet and crumpled slips of paper, he tore it open with shaking hands.

Finding those trembling fingers endearing, Val sat up and helped him put the protection in place. He cupped her face in his hands and locked his gaze to hers as he laid her back again.

"I love you, Val," he whispered, "and you won't be sorry again, I swear."

Tears clouded her eyes and clogged her throat as she welcomed him back into her body and heart.

Chapter Sixteen

Ian arrived at the fire scene, stopped the truck at a safe distance and got out, reaching for the protective coveralls that he had taken to carrying with him everywhere he went. A low, long blaze had eaten away about half an acre of tall, yellow grass in the empty pasture. He'd never seen anything like the spate of fires this season had brought. Each one was different: a cigarette tossed carelessly aside, an oily barn fire, an electrical short in a storage unit, a trash Dumpster into which books and books of matches had been discarded, and now another grass fire. Ian felt in his bones that these fires were somehow related, but the damage had been minimal so far, and he'd found nothing to definitely link them.

The whir of tires on gravel had him turning his head as he dragged on his work boots. Buddy Wilcox bailed out in full battle regalia. Ian couldn't deny that Buddy had matured as a firefighter. He responded quickly when the call went out, was even the first to show on several occasions, and Ian had to admit that his skills had improved. Buddy had even taken to showing up at meetings and on training days. No piker when it came to praising his force, especially since it was largely a volunteer one, Ian made sure to compliment Buddy from time to time, and the two seemed to have developed an uneasy but tenable working relationship; yet Ian couldn't quite trust the man. Of course, the way he tried to maneuver Val into private conversation could have a lot to do with that.

Buddy hoisted a shovel from the back of his battered car, shouting, "I'll take the north edge."

Nodding, Ian grabbed his own shovel and trotted toward the end of the fire line opposite Buddy. The line had already begun to curve. If they could reinforce that tendency, sharpen the curve, it would drive the most aggressive part of the flames to the road, where it would die a natural death, barring any sudden rise in the wind. He began the backbreaking, lung-searing work of throwing dirt on the flickering flames.

By the time the water truck and a three-man crew arrived some ten minutes later, he and Buddy had the fire line under control. Val rolled up a few minutes after the water truck with a keg of ice water in the trunk of her car. She had become a fixture on-site these past weeks, and a welcome one.

Ian leaned on his shovel, wiped sweat from his forehead and glanced toward the opposite edge of the fire line. Buddy was already trudging toward Val's car. Ian followed suit. Being closer, he got there before Buddy and was standing next to her, draining the cup she'd handed him when Buddy finally arrived. Knowing he could afford to be generous, he gave Buddy his due.

"Good work, Wilcox. Maybe it's time you were running your own squad."

Buddy slid Valerie a pointed look before accepting the cup she offered him. "Thanks." He gulped down the water, sighed and looked to Val once more. "How're you doing?"

"Good."

"Family okay?"

"Fine, thanks."

"Don't see you out and about much anymore. Everybody misses you."

Valerie smiled. "I'm pretty busy these days."

He glanced at Ian, nodded, tossed the empty cup into a box placed for that purpose in the trunk of her car and turned away, going back to the fire, though the water crew had it well under control.

Valerie muttered thoughtfully, "He just might amount to something yet."

"Yeah," Ian said, but he wondered. Something about Buddy felt forced, dishonest. Then again, it was probably just his jealousy talking. Buddy's continued interest in Val was obvious, and Ian couldn't help thinking from time to time that theirs was a long and convoluted history. Then he remembered what it felt like going to sleep with her in his arms, and smiled to himself. They'd spent the night at his place last night, and he could honestly say that he'd never slept so well as he had with her in his bed.

"Better help them mop up."

She nodded and leaned a hip against the fender of the car, settling in to wait until he was finished. Ian got back to business, but a part of him stayed with Valerie. He had come to understand that a part of him always would. He was also coming to realize how foolish it was to fight the inevitable. He had clung to old ideas far too long, none of which applied now. Valerie had changed everything, and no matter what he'd said to Warren in the heat of the moment, he knew that he wouldn't truly have it any other way.

He looked at her, leaning there against the car, just waiting. For him. And he knew that he didn't need any more time. He only needed her.

"Ian, is that you?"

Sierra Carlton emerged from the back of the florist's shop and grinned at him over the head of the woman at the counter. This was a more polished Sierra than Ian had ever seen. The braid was gone, replaced by a tail of lustrous red hair that emerged from the center of an intricate knot just below her right ear. Slim, cropped pants and a short, form-fitting knit top of vibrant turquoise called attention to her svelte figure. Understated makeup brightened her pretty, squarish face and made the most of her prominent bone structure. She looked polished and prosperous and confident, and Ian smiled with genuine pleasure.

"I didn't expect to see you here."

She laid a hand on the heavy shoulder of the shorter

woman. "Bette has decided that she'd rather work for me than lease the shop on her own. It's always been too much for one person or even two, really."

"Sierra's good to keep it open just because I need the work," Bette said, her plain, round face earnest. As wide as she was tall and at least five years Sierra's senior, she wore an air of good-natured innocence weighted by hardship. With a worshipful glance at her employer, she pushed away from the counter, saying, "I'd best check the refrigerators. He wants a dozen red roses."

Sierra smiled knowingly. "Yes, I heard that. A dozen of our finest, I believe he said."

"I think we have that many good ones," Bette muttered as she disappeared behind the curtain.

Sierra sighed. "It's difficult to get good inventory out here. I do better driving into Dallas and picking up my blooms at the wholesale market there, but that's a pain, I can tell you."

"Well, at least your livelihood no longer depends on it," Ian said encouragingly.

Sierra leaned close and in a low voice revealed, "No, now it's Bette's livelihood and the young woman's she hired to help out part-time before she decided that she couldn't make a go of the place on her own. Instead of me and my child depending on this shop, now it's two women and four children."

Ian blew out a sympathetic breath. "So your responsibilities have quadrupled, essentially."

Sierra leaned a slender hip against the counter and folded her arms. "Sometimes I wish Edwin Searle had died penniless. It was a day-to-day struggle, you know, but it was familiar, comfortable. So much has changed now. I've barely talked to Avis, Val and Gwyn in weeks, and I've heard way too much from Heston Witt.''

Ian frowned. ''Is he still trying to make trouble for you?''

''Valerie hasn't told you?''

Ian frowned. ''No.''

''Well, maybe it doesn't bother her as much as it does me. It's just the kinds of things he's saying, you know.''

''Such as?''

She shrugged. ''He's been spreading rumors about us, all sorts of talk. In my case it's that I've been disinherited by my father because of my supposedly seamy past. I've even heard that my daughter's father and I were never married, that I don't even know who her father is.''

''What rot.''

''He's gone around saying that Avis is a home wrecker and that she cheated her late husband's real family of their rightful inheritance when he died.''

Ian rolled his eyes. ''Yeah, like she was set up for life before Edwin left her a fortune.''

''Exactly. Still, people are all too willing to listen to that junk, more willing now than ever where the three of us are concerned.''

Ian nodded his understanding and waited, but she didn't say anything more. ''You going to tell me what rumor he's spreading about Val?''

Sierra looked down. After a moment she answered succinctly, ''Town slut. He's painting her as a party girl who's been around the block one too many times.''

Ian felt heat explode upward from his chest to the top of his head. For a moment he couldn't see anything but red. Finally he got himself in hand enough to speak. ''We'll see about that.''

''Don't do anything rash,'' Sierra counseled him. ''Corbett says we can sue him for slander if we can prove he's the source of these rumors, but if you ask me that would just keep it all stirred up.''

Ian nodded. ''You're probably right.''

It was as well, he supposed that he'd finally accepted that marriage was the only way for him and Val. She'd become such an integral part of his existence that he could hardly bear that they were basically still living in two places. Oh, he could probably talk her into living with him. He'd even told himself that it was the next logical step, but it wasn't what he wanted for them. Simply put, he had to marry the woman. Nothing else would do. Tonight he would convince her of that, and after it was settled with the two of them, he just might have to pay a call on Heston Witt. First things first, however.

''About those roses,'' he said to Sierra, reaching into his hip pocket.

She smiled knowingly. ''Ah, yes, the roses. Some special occasion is it?''

He nodded happily. ''You could say that.''

''Would there, perhaps, be a jeweler involved in this special occasion?''

Ian simply grinned. Sierra reached across the counter and patted his arm.

"Val's a lucky girl."

"No, I'm the lucky one," he said, suddenly feeling short of breath. "I hope." His insides were quivering again. They'd been doing that off and on ever since he'd decided that tonight was *the* night.

Bette pushed through the curtain just then, a huge bouquet of long-stemmed, blood red roses wrapped in green paper in her arms. "These ought to do the trick," she announced proudly. "I only had to peel a few petals."

Ian flopped open his wallet and paid for the bouquet, insisting on coughing up the full price even though Sierra would have given him the roses at cost.

"She's worth it," he said, signing the credit card receipt.

"Yeah, she is," Sierra agreed. "I'm glad you realized it."

"I may be slow, but I'm not dumb," he said, leaving her with a wink and a smile.

The quivering in his gut eased, and a feeling of lightness, elation, swelled his chest as he carried the heavy bouquet from the shop to his truck. He carefully positioned the roses on the seat beside him, then opened the dash compartment and removed the small, blue velvet box that he had placed there earlier. After taking another look at the ring inside, reassuring himself that it was the largest diamond he could afford, he started up the truck and headed over to Valerie's apartment, mentally rehearsing his proposal.

He had just slowed and turned into the apartment building parking lot when the twin radios on his belt and visor chirruped.

"Fire One, come in. This is Dispatch."

Biting off a curse word, Ian stomped the truck to a halt and snagged the radio on his belt. "Fire One here. This had better be routine."

"Afraid not," came the unwelcome message. "We've got a bad one this time, Marshal. Downtown on the square."

The ominous portent of that slammed into Ian. The buildings on the square snugged together, sometimes wall to wall, occasionally with a few feet or yards between them behind the facades. A fire in one building on such a block was considered a fire in the whole block, and for very good reason. The entire downtown area could go up. Even more troubling was the fire itself, or rather, this latest in a series of fires that Ian was convinced had been intentionally set.

He keyed the mic, resigned and alarmed. "We're going to need help. Call the Granbury, Cleburne and Burleson departments. Ask for all possible backup. I'm on my way."

He glanced at the second-story door behind which Valerie surely sat waiting and regretfully yanked the truck into gear. Best laid plans. Reaching for the little blue box, he tossed it back into the glove compartment and slammed the lid. The roses he could do nothing about. As for Val, he'd call her later. If he called her now, she'd just show up at the fire scene, and if this was the bad one he'd been anticipating, he didn't want her there, not this time. Better she should stay safe, even if it made her mad. Determinedly turning his mind from that, he mentally shoved aside his deep disappointment and began playing out in his head the job at hand.

Valerie punched the correct button and lifted the telephone receiver to her ear. "Ian?"

"You've heard then." The voice, while familiar, was not, unfortunately, masculine.

"Gwyn? Heard what?"

"About the fire. They're saying the whole square could go up any minute."

"The square?" Val's heart thudded. This was bad, very bad. Suddenly chilled to the bone, Valerie got up and walked to the front door, throwing it open. The distant wail of sirens rode in on a wave of summer heat, bringing the taste of ash with it.

"Thanks for calling, Gwyn. I've got to go now."

"Let me know when you hear from him, will you?"

"Sure." Not that she intended to wait for his call.

Switching off the phone, she returned it to its cradle, then hurriedly traded her shorts for jeans and slung on a lightweight, long-sleeved cotton blouse. She'd learned a thing or two over these past weeks. Sparks could be flying up close. And that was exactly where she intended to be.

She'd have done better to leave her car parked at the apartment building, Val though irritably, turning the coupe into her mother's drive. Every road into and out of downtown Puma Springs was blocked. Ian had warned her that would be the case if a fire were serious enough, which only served to reinforce her fear and her determination. Delores waved from the front yard, where several of the neighbors had gathered to watch the column of black smoke climbing the dusky blue sky.

"They say Kraven's is burning," Delores announced without preamble as Valerie exited the car.

Valerie felt a shiver of fear. Kraven's Collectibles billed itself as an antique store, and a portion of the ground floor was given over to old furniture, but the vast majority of the goods crammed into the old two-story building was nothing more than junk—highly flammable junk, everything from used magazines, comic books and posters to old clothes and textile products. The store was a bonfire just waiting for a match to ignite it.

"Wait here, Mama," she said, moving toward the sidewalk.

"You can't really get any closer," one of her mother's neighbors said.

"I can," Val said confidently, walking with a sure, purposeful stride. She wasn't Ian Keene's woman for nothing, by golly.

Five blocks later, she came upon a small crowd milling around a barricade in the car-lined street. A policeman leaned against it, chatting with some of the people watching the smoke and waiting for news. Valerie cut behind a hedge, circled around a house and slipped along a narrow alley to its end, then calmly walked between two buildings to the corner of the downtown square. A few people stood on the sidewalks watching the activity across the greensward where the church stood, but otherwise the street seemed eerily empty. Well past business hours, the day was beginning to fade toward night, aided by the heavy, gray pall of smoke pouring upward from the center of the block opposite her. Valerie felt the pit drop out of her stomach as she hurried across the green, weaving between the gravestones.

Up close the scene was one of controlled chaos, with men running this way and that, dragging hoses and hefting axes. Those in uniform had radios affixed to the shoulders of their coats. Streams of water arced through the air into the building. A ladder truck had been pulled right up onto the sidewalk, and Val had spied a so-called cherry picker at the back of the building while still at a distance, its bucket hovering over the flat roof. An unfamiliar man with stripes on his sleeves hailed her.

"Ma'am, this area is restricted. You have to leave the area."

Before she could say a word on her own behalf, one of the members of Ian's volunteer force spoke up in her defense. "That's all right, man. She's with the chief."

The other man shrugged and walked away. Her defender hurried on to whatever chore awaited him. Valerie followed after glancing around but failed to catch sight of Ian. "Hey. Hey! Where is he? Where is Ian?"

"Haven't seen him lately," flew over his shoulder.

Valerie turned back, only to walk straight into the arms of Buddy Wilcox. "Thought you'd be here," he said, smiling down at her.

She had to admit that he looked handsome rigged out in what Ian referred to as "battle gear." A shock of wheat-brown hair fell forward across his forehead under the brim of his hat, and a wide smear of soot decorated one cheek, calling attention to his pale, gray-blue eyes and giving him a manly air. Completely unmoved, Valerie gripped him by the upper arms.

"Have you seen Ian?"

Buddy tilted his head. "Tell me something, Val. What's he got that I don't? Is it the job? Because I could have the job, you know."

"Don't be ridiculous," she snapped impatiently.

"I could," Buddy insisted. "I'm squad leader now, and I've always been popular in this town. Everybody says I could have his job if I wanted it."

She didn't have time to argue with him. The idea that Buddy could replace Ian in any way was laughable, but her only concern at the moment was making sure that Ian was okay. She didn't have to speak to him or even see him. She just needed to find someone who could tell her that he was safe.

"Whatever you say, Buddy. Look, I need to know where Ian is."

A shower of sparks rained down on their heads. They ducked and threw up their arms, scurrying farther back as someone shouted, "Get our men off that roof!" someone else yelled.

Suddenly Buddy's hand fell on her shoulder. "It's going to cave," he said, "and Ian's in there." Val felt the ground shift under her feet. "Don't worry," he went on, moving off. "I'll find him for you."

It didn't occur to her to protest, to even think of Buddy's safety. All she cared about was Ian being inside a burning building with the roof about to collapse. What if she should lose him?

"Oh, God." She stumbled backward and nearly fell over a hose, her eyes never leaving the burning building. Two firefighters, one a woman, passed by her at a run. A bell began clanging. Val barely registered any of it. After a moment, she realized that she was praying aloud.

"Oh, God, please. Let him be all right. My life's nothing without him. Nothing means anything without him. The money means nothing without him. I'll give it all away. I'll even give it to Heston if You want. Just please, please let him be safe."

An eternity passed. Someone touched her on the shoulder. She whirled to find an old friend, sooty, sweaty and begrimed in full fire-fighting regalia.

"Skeet!" The bartender at the steak house.

"Are you okay?"

She didn't know how to answer that, so instead she attempted an explanation. "Ian." Since that was all she could get out, she pointed to the burning building. "B-Buddy!"

Skeet frowned. "What about Buddy?"

"H-he went in a-after Ian."

With a look of alarm, Skeet started running. A low, plaintive whine had her looking down.

"Cato." She dropped down to a crouch beside the big, black dog. "Where is Ian? Oh, you're worried about him, too." She looped her arms about the thick, furred neck. The dog *whuffed*, then barked sharply, just once.

Someone screamed, "Get back! Get back!"

Valerie couldn't have moved if she'd wanted to. Her whole being and that of the animal with her were concentrated on that burning building.

Ian. Oh, God, Ian.

She hadn't told him that she loved him since they'd gotten back together. She hadn't told him that he was more important to her than anything else in the world, that being with him, any way he wanted her, was all that counted.

An ominous creak rumbled from the building. Someone yelled, "The second floor is caving in!" Valerie watched, immobilized with fear as white smoke gathered low against the gray-black sky and spilled from the upper windows, behind which flames flickered and danced. Beside her, the dog quivered.

Her heart, her life began crumbling right before her eyes.

Chapter Seventeen

Valerie felt a scream building inside her. She curled her hands into fists in an effort to keep it inside. Seconds crawled by, each its own agonizing eternity, as a low rumble built to a roar. The white cloud billowing inside the building now pushed through the tops of the first floor windows and, finally, the door. Even as her heart leapt into her throat, Val sank to her knees, but Cato barked, suddenly alert. Valerie sharpened her gaze and caught sight of faint movement in the center of that dense white cloud now flowing toward her.

"Medic!" shouted a familiar voice. "We need a medic!" The dog bolted forward, and Valerie rose on legs shaky with relief. He was alive. Hurt or not, Ian was alive and giving orders. "Get a stretcher in here!"

She lurched to her feet and started moving stiffly forward, coughing as the gritty smog reached her. A large, undulating, misshapen figure materialized out of the swirling smoke. A moment later Valerie realized that she was looking at one man carrying another over his right shoulder, both fully outfitted in heavy, protective clothing, as a big, black dog cavorted around them. The walker still wore his hard hat with the elongated bill in the back and a filter mask over his mouth and nose. He carried the second man over his shoulder easily, a small ax swinging from his left hand. She instinctively recognized him. Ian. Her love. Her heart.

He strode out of the swirling fog of smoke and dust like a conquering warlord, every step a sure, unhurried piece of work. When he spied her, he reached up and tore the filter mask from his face, leaving it dangling from one ear.

Valerie gave a glad cry and broke into a run. His face was grim and filthy above the clean patch left by the mask, but he smiled, tossed down the ax and lifted his arm in welcome. She plastered herself to his side, pressed her face into the crook of his neck. He smelled of smoke and rubber and Ian. Cato *whuffed* and ran ahead, tail sweeping rhythmically in a wide arc. Tears spilled from her eyes.

''Thank God. Oh, thank God!''

He clasped her tight as a pair of burly emergency medical technicians ran up, collapsed stretcher and kit in tow. ''What's the story?''

''Broken left leg,'' Ian told them. ''Maybe a light concussion.''

They popped the wheels on the stretcher and placed it on the ground. "What happened?"

"Don't know for sure. I found him in the rear of the building under some fallen debris."

Valerie forced herself to let go of Ian and step aside as he carefully lowered the injured firefighter to the narrow stretcher. Valerie gasped as Buddy Wilcox writhed and groaned, clawing at his filter mask. Ian reached out for her again as pounding footsteps sounded behind them. Cato took up a protective stance beside Ian, staring back into the haze. Skeet rushed out of the smoke, paused to catch his breath, bending forward slightly at the waist, then ran straight to the stretcher, seizing Buddy by the front of his slicker.

"You stupid son of a—!"

"Hey, man!" Buddy shouted, squirming away. "I'm hurt here. I got hit by a falling pipe looking for him." He pointed at Ian.

"Why were you looking for me?" Ian asked, sounding puzzled. "You knew I was canvassing the building. You told me you heard voices in the office area."

Buddy's gaze zipped from face to face. "I did. Earlier."

"How much earlier?" Ian wanted to know as the emergency medical technicians opened their bag and began removing instruments.

Before Buddy could answer, Skeet accused, "You weren't looking for anyone!" He turned to Ian. "I saw exactly what happened. I went around back to find you, let you know that Val was here. I saw him

standing right outside the building, cooling his heels
in what he obviously thought was a safe place. Then
the building caved and the plumbing smokestack top-
pled over the edge of the roof. It hit him and knocked
him right through the door into the building.''

"That's a lie!" Buddy exclaimed, and one of the
EMTs pushed him down on his back and threw a strap
across his chest, ordering him to be still. Buddy
looked to Valerie, pleading, "I was looking for him,
I swear. I just went out there to get a breath of air.''

"After you told me that you'd heard voices in the
office area," Ian stated pointedly.

At the same time, Skeet said to Buddy, "I know
what you've been doing, man.''

"I haven't been doing anything!" Buddy insisted,
wincing as the EMTs began checking him over.

"He's been setting fires," Skeet said to Ian. "One
of his pals told me last night over one too many
beers.''

Ian sighed and admitted, "I suspected it.''

"That's not true!" Buddy wailed, but Valerie knew
the truth when she heard it. She looked to Buddy in
confusion.

"Why, Buddy? What were you thinking?''

"He wanted to be a hero," Skeet said, spitting the
words out with disgust. "He was playing out of his
league, trying to compete with Ian.''

"He was trying to get you back," Ian said, tightening the arm he had looped about her waist.

"She was my girl first!" Buddy yelled, fending off
an EMT who was trying to listen to his chest with a

stethoscope. "She was always my girl until you came along!" Deep coughs convulsed him.

"I was never your girl," Valerie told him. "That's just something I let you believe from time to time, Buddy, but I was never yours, and you never tried very hard to keep me until I had money."

"Oh, like the money means nothing to him!"

"That's right," Valerie said. "The money means nothing to him."

"Nothing whatsoever," Ian affirmed. "In fact, before we're married I'm going to insist on an ironclad prenup."

Valerie's head whipped around at the word "married." She barely heard Buddy whining, "Val, you're not gonna marry him, are you? Not after everything I've done to show you how much I care about you!"

Ian pulled his gaze from Valerie's and targeted Buddy. "Just what *have* you done, Wilcox? Did you set this fire?"

Buddy literally paled. "No! No, I swear I didn't. I—I only set the small ones. I was real careful, made sure nothing was really lost, that nobody got hurt."

"I think we better get a cop over here," the EMT muttered darkly, poking the unused stethoscope back into the open bag.

"No!" Buddy screamed. "It was just little stuff, stuff that didn't matter to anyone." Seeing that he was winning no sympathy from the fire marshal, he turned to Valerie. "I did it for *you*."

Valerie shook her head. "You didn't do anything for me. I doubt you've ever done anything for anyone but yourself."

"You want me to find a policeman?" Skeet asked Ian.

Ian glanced at Valerie, then shook his head. "No. I'll take care of it." He glanced at Buddy and added, "He's not going anywhere."

"Just to the hospital," the EMT said, unlocking the wheels of the stretcher.

"I didn't hurt anybody," Buddy complained. "Isn't a broken leg enough punishment?"

"Not if you tried to hurt the marshal today," Skeet said, "and I think you did."

Buddy set his jaw mulishly as the two male technicians began rolling the stretcher across the pavement toward a waiting ambulance. Valerie felt the skin prickle on the back of her neck.

"I should've told you today what I'd heard," Skeet was saying to Ian, "but I figured it would be better coming from the guy who told me, so I tried to convince him to go to you instead."

Ian nodded. "Right now all that matters is the job. We can still use your help containing this blaze. We'll get into this other matter later."

"Okay. Whatever you say." Skeet moved off.

Ian finally turned his full attention to Valerie, folding her tight against him. "You're not supposed to be anywhere near here."

"Yeah, well."

He chuckled. "Yeah. Well." He looked down. "I've gotten you all dirty."

She smiled. "I don't care. All I care about, if you must know, is you."

"I want to know," he said softly, his gaze targeting

her mouth, but then he glanced around them and sighed before dipping down slightly to rub and pat Cato. The big dog sat, looked up adoringly and laid his big head against Ian's thigh. Val knew just how the devoted animal felt.

"Ian, do you really think Buddy was trying to hurt you? Did he send you to that office hoping the building was going to fall in on your head?"

"I don't know," Ian answered, looking up at her. "I doubt he knew the roof was ready to give. Maybe he just wanted to keep me away from you. Speaking of which, you've got to get away to a safe distance and let me go back work."

She swallowed down a spurt of worry mixed with disappointment. That marriage remark would have to go unexplored for now. Such was the lot of a fire-fighter's woman. She squared her shoulders. "You'll be careful?"

He gave her a lopsided grin. "Never more so, but not to worry. The worst is over. We've got several more hours' work here, but it's just mop up, really." She nodded and began backing away. "Cato," Ian ordered, straightening, "go with Val. Go with Val." The big dog stood and padded after Valerie.

"I'll, uh, be at my mother's," she called.

"Okay. By the way, if you happen to pass by my truck, there's something for you on the front seat."

She lifted her eyebrows at that and looked around her until she located Ian's pickup parked in front of the church. When she looked back again, he was gone. *"Before we're married,"* he had said, as thoughtlessly as if he'd said it every day for weeks. Maybe he had, inside his heart, where it counted most.

"Well," Heston Witt said in his best mayoral voice, "this is a fine mess." True to form, he hadn't shown up until the danger was well past and only then to look down his nose, at everyone and everything. Ian was in no mood, especially after what he'd heard from Sierra that afternoon. That seemed days ago now.

"Actually, it's a whole lot less of a mess than it could have been," Ian told him tiredly.

"It's completely destroyed!" Heston insisted, jabbing a finger at the burned out building.

"One building is destroyed," Ian said. "With a fire like this one, it's better than even money that the whole row will go, especially in a town with a department made up mainly of volunteers. All in all, we did darn well here today."

Heston folded his hands officiously. "You would say so, of course, if only to cover your own hide. Well, I have to answer to the constituency, and the good citizens of Puma Springs are entitled to a fire marshal who would actually put out fires and not let them burn buildings to the ground. I'm afraid I'm going to have to withdraw my support, Keene. This is gross dereliction of duty on your part."

"Oh, put a sock in it, Heston," Ian snapped. "Your support means nothing to me or anyone else around here, and your threats have more to do with Edwin's will and the three women than someone else's fire damage."

"Those three...well, I can't even describe them politely, those three...they don't deserve that money. He was *my* uncle."

"And he despised you," Ian said bluntly, "because you treated him so badly."

"That's not true! Those connivers alienated his affections from me."

"Is that your tale now?" Ian asked, his voice thick with scorn. "You couldn't sell that stupidity boxed in solid gold."

"We'll see about that!"

Ian looked around him. Action on the busy street had come to an almost complete halt. Uniformed firemen from three cities had stopped coiling their hoses and tallying smoke masks and performing a dozen other tasks to watch the little drama unfolding in their midst. Ian decided it was a good place to take a stand.

"No, we won't," he told his honor sternly, shaking a finger in Heston's doughy face, "because it's a bald-faced lie. You treated your uncle like dirt because he wouldn't hand over the family ranch to you, and you only found this great love for him after he was cold in the ground and you realized he also had several million bucks in the bank! Meanwhile, those three hardworking women you're so jealous of were taking the time to treat a lonely old man with kindness and understanding, never realizing that he had an extra penny to his name. I don't blame Edwin for leaving his money to them, especially considering the kind of filthy tales you've been spreading about them. And I'm telling you now, Heston, that if you don't leave Valerie and her friends alone, I'll be coming after you.''

''You can't threaten me!''

''That's not a threat, Heston. That's a promise. Open your nasty mouth one more time to spread another of your rumors and you're going to have a little meeting with my fists. Do you understand me?''

Heston's eyes went wide as saucers, and he scrambled backward as if fearing Ian would introduce him to those ham-hock fists of his right there on the spot. Spying a fireman standing nearby, Heston hurried over to him. ''He threatened me. You heard him. You're a witness. You heard him!''

The man just shook his head and turned away with an expression of disgust.

Desperate now, Heston raised his voice. ''You all heard it! The marshal threatened me because I called him to account for the job he did here today!''

Brent stepped forward then, so exhausted his knuckles were practically dragging the ground. ''Every man here will swear that the marshal did an excellent job this day,'' he announced loudly. A chorus of agreement wafted around the square. ''I don't know anyone who could've done better. As for that other nonsense, if it was my woman you were ragging on, I'd have already made your dentist a rich man.''

''Put him in traction would be more like it,'' someone else said.

''Or the ground,'' proclaimed another.

Heston's already-pale complexion drained of all color. Then he turned and scurried away. Ian smiled to himself.

"Thanks, boys," he said loud enough for all to hear.

Brent saluted lazily. "No problem, boss."

Boss. Ian's chest swelled with pride. In his, their, old unit, "boss" had been a title of respect, almost an endearment, hard won and always well deserved. He knew Brent was tired, and he knew as well that the stocky redhead wouldn't leave the site until the last piece of gear was stowed and the last truck had rolled out of town.

"Think you can handle this? I've got something important to do."

"Sure thing."

"After that, you go on home," Ian ordered. "I'll get one of the other men to handle your watch tonight."

Brent grinned. "Now that's a deal, and after she says yes, we'll celebrate."

Ian dropped his shoulders, dumbfounded. "How did you know?"

"I saw the roses on the seat of your truck, and I heard you were seen in a certain jewelry store earlier."

Ian shook his head, chuckling. Such was life in a small town. Might as well get used to it. He wasn't going anywhere, not up, not out, not away. This was his town now. Home.

She was sitting on her mother's front porch step, flanked by a vase of drooping red roses and a big, lolling, black dog when he came clomping up the sidewalk. They were a little worse for wear, those roses, but she thought they were the most beautiful things she'd ever seen—other than the man dragging up the front walk in heavy, blunt-toed boots and sooty yellow overalls. Smoke and soot had dyed the once-white T-shirt beneath the wide, black suspenders a dingy gray. His face looked like a fright mask, and though he'd combed his perspiration-dampened hair with his fingers, it looked rumpled and dirty. He was the very picture of her heart's desire.

She was pretty grimy herself, at least her blouse was, and her mother had declared that her hair and clothes smelled of smoke and tar. Val couldn't have cared less. She rose as he drew near, Cato scrambling up beside her. Then, as he moved close enough, she lifted her arms, tipped herself forward and literally allowed herself to fall against him, arms winding about his neck. He locked his own arms in the small of her back and hauled her up hard. She hung there against him, her feet dangling above the ground, while Cato panted with doggy delight.

Their mouths came together. He turned in a slow circle, while she soaked in the feel and smell and taste of him. Finally, he pulled his head back, smiled apologetically and said, "I blew it."

"No, you didn't."

"Yeah, I did. I wanted to make a grand, romantic proposal, and instead it just slipped out in the heat of the moment."

Her heart fluttered. Tears rose in her eyes. "It doesn't matter."

"If it sounded like I was taking your answer for granted, I'm sorry," he went on. "I—I just can't let myself think that you'll refuse me. I love you, Val, and I was a fool to think that anything less than marriage would be enough for me where you're concerned.''

She tucked her face into the curve of his neck and just sobbed, overcome with joy.

"Oh, honey, don't,'' he begged. "You're scaring me.'' Cato rose up and added his weight to the plea, nearly knocking them over.

She chuckled, lifted her head, wiped black streaks across her face, patted Cato and said to Ian, "Nothing scares you.''

"Sure it does.''

"Ha. You walk through fire and falling buildings like you were strolling through a park.''

"Fire and falling debris are just part of the job,'' he said solemnly. "The thought of losing you, that scares me half to death.''

"You couldn't lose me,'' she told him honestly. "Even if you never wanted to marry me, I'm afraid I'd be hanging around your neck from now on.''

He laughed. It was a rich, happy sound that thrilled her right down to her toes. "I do want to marry you, though, more than I even realized until just now.''

"I want to marry you, too,'' she whispered, touching the tip of her nose to his.

One corner of his mouth kicked up. "In that case,'' he said, a lascivious gleam in his sky blue eyes, "I'd better give you a bath so I can make wild, passionate love to you.''

It was her turn to laugh, but as he swept her legs

up and prepared to carry her away in his arms, she twisted and pointed to the porch. "My roses!"

He rolled his eyes, but he turned around and bent forward, so she could scoop the vase into her arms. Cato took advantage, swiping her cheek with his tongue. "Cato, heel!" Ian ordered, turning toward the street.

"I have something else for you," he informed her as he carried her toward his house, "something that will outlast the roses."

She gasped and looped one arm around his neck. "A ring?"

"It's just a single karat," he warned. "I can't really afford more than that right now, but if you think it's not big enough, I'll—"

Whatever else he might have said was lost in her kiss. He stopped, let her body fall down against his and devoted himself to the pleasure, the wonder, of it. Cato, wisely, dropped down to sprawl at their feet.

The world could get lost in such kisses and frequently would, for they shared such a wealth of them, these two. They were the richest couple in town, and as Edwin had known, it had nothing at all to do with money. Real wealth couldn't be held by banks and trust funds and vaults. Real treasure could only be held in the hearts of those who loved unreservedly. Valerie had finally claimed her true legacy, and it was one in which Ian owned an equal share, after all.

*   *   *   *   *

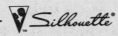

SPECIAL EDITION™

Three small-town women have their lives turned
upside down by a sudden inheritance.
Change is good, but change this big?

Richest Gals in Texas

by Arlene James

BEAUTICIAN GETS MILLION-DOLLAR TIP!

(Silhouette Special Edition #1589,
available January 2004)

A sexy commitment-shy fire marshal meets his match
in a beautician with big...bucks?

FORTUNE FINDS FLORIST

(Silhouette Special Edition #1596,
available February 2004)

It's time to get down and dirty when a beautiful
florist teams up with a sexy farmer....

TYCOON MEETS TEXAN!

(Silhouette Special Edition #1601,
available March 2004)

The trip of a lifetime turns into something more
when a widow is swept off her feet by someone
tall, dark and wealthy....

Available at your favorite retail outlet.

If you enjoyed what you just read,
then we've got an offer you can't resist!

Take 2 bestselling
love stories FREE!
Plus get a FREE surprise gift!

Clip this page and mail it to Silhouette Reader Service™

IN U.S.A.	IN CANADA
3010 Walden Ave.	P.O. Box 609
P.O. Box 1867	Fort Erie, Ontario
Buffalo, N.Y. 14240-1867	L2A 5X3

YES! Please send me 2 free Silhouette Special Edition® novels and my free surprise gift. After receiving them, if I don't wish to receive anymore, I can return the shipping statement marked cancel. If I don't cancel, I will receive 6 brand-new novels every month, before they're available in stores! In the U.S.A., bill me at the bargain price of $3.99 plus 25¢ shipping and handling per book and applicable sales tax, if any*. In Canada, bill me at the bargain price of $4.74 plus 25¢ shipping and handling per book and applicable taxes**. That's the complete price and a savings of at least 10% off the cover prices—what a great deal! I understand that accepting the 2 free books and gift places me under no obligation ever to buy any books. I can always return a shipment and cancel at any time. Even if I never buy another book from Silhouette, the 2 free books and gift are mine to keep forever.

235 SDN DNUR
335 SDN DNUS

Name	(PLEASE PRINT)	
Address	Apt.#	
City	State/Prov.	Zip/Postal Code

* Terms and prices subject to change without notice. Sales tax applicable in N.Y.
** Canadian residents will be charged applicable provincial taxes and GST.
All orders subject to approval. Offer limited to one per household and not valid to current Silhouette Special Edition® subscribers.
® are registered trademarks of Harlequin Books S.A., used under license.

SPED02   ©1998 Harlequin Enterprises Limited

eHARLEQUIN.com

Your favorite authors are just a click away
at www.eHarlequin.com!

- Take our **Sister Author Quiz** and
  we'll match you up with the author
  most like you!

- Choose from over 500
  author **profiles!**

- Chat with your favorite authors
  on our **message boards.**

- Are you an author in the making?
  Get advice from published authors
  in **The Inside Scoop!**

- Get the latest on **author appearances**
  and tours!

**Want to know more about your
favorite romance authors?**

Choose from over 500 author profiles!

Learn about your favorite authors
in a fun, interactive setting—
visit www.eHarlequin.com today!

INTAUTH

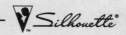

SPECIAL EDITION™

presents

DOWN FROM THE MOUNTAIN
by Barbara Gale
(Silhouette Special Edition #1595)

Carrying scars from his youth, forest ranger
David Hartwell had fled his home and settled in
the sanctuary of the Adirondack mountains.
But now, called back to deal with his father's will,
he was faced with temporary guardianship of
Ellen Candler—beautiful, innocent and exactly
the kind of woman David had always avoided.

Only, this time he
couldn't run away.

Because Ellen was blind.

And she needed him.

Follow the journey of
these two extraordinary
people as they leave their
sheltered existences behind
to embrace life and love!

Available February 2004 at your favorite retail outlet.

Visit Silhouette at www.eHarlequin.com   SSEDFTM

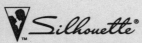
Silhouette®

COMING NEXT MONTH

SSECNM0104